Tales From the Frozen North

A Moorhead Friends Writing

Group Anthology

This is a work of fiction. Names, characters, places, and incidents either are the product of the author's imagination or are used fictitiously. Any resemblance to actual persons, living or dead, events,or locales is entirely coincidental.

Copyright 2022

First Paperback Edition April 2022

Edited by Robin Pope Cain

Cover Design by Tiffany Fier

Cover Photo by Shelia Skogen

ISBN 979-8985885217 (paperback)

ISBN 979-8985885200 (ebook)

Published by Moorhead Friends Writing Group

Table of Contents

A Cold You Couldn't Forget

By Amy Scheibe

"Did you grow up in an igloo?" No, a trailer house.

"Aren't there like, ten people in North Dakota?" Actually, only nine. I left.

"Everyone's related there, right?" Yes, that's why I left, so I didn't have to marry my cousin.

"I bet you had a pet cow." Only fools name their food.

"You must not feel the cold, being from the tundra." We went from warm house to warm car to overheated school to warm car to chilly grocery store to warm car to slowly-warming church to warm car. I maybe spent a cumulative 10 hours in 18 years in below zero temps. Five minutes at a time.

"Amy's the only person I've ever met from South Dakota." North. Dakota.

"Did you learn in a one-room schoolhouse?" You're joking, right? No? Then, no. Think Hoosiers. With more snow.

"You're pretty smart for someone born in North Dakota." I was born in Minnesota. Not to confuse you.

"What was it like growing up with those people?"

I moved away from the Upper Midwest three decades ago, resettling on the East Coast. Over the years the questions have changed, reflecting the times, and the cultural sway of ignorance about people who come from the edge of the middle of nowhere. What remains the same is the smug assurance that being born in the eccentric center of America somehow marks you for derision. It's perfectly fine to passively bully someone about being a "flyover," especially if that someone has chosen to leave the set of Green Acres and outwardly realign their associations with an East Coast swagger. It's survival. Eat or be eaten. But I never joined in the jokes, never let down my guard, or became absorbed by the Red Rover line of self-appointed arbiters of everything acceptable. Instead, I dug in my heels, set my jaw, and honored my upbringing by depicting its complexity through the written word.

In these pages, you will discover many birds of this feather, who know what it's like to sing in a choir in a church basement on a Saturday in December, or how to assemble the exact number of layers to be readily comfortable in any house, car, or building. You'll also begin to realize that to "be from" a place that is cold even when it's 100 degrees in the July shade takes a certain kind of character, a backbone, a resilience that exists in that slow beat, that pause between when a question is asked in jest and then answered in unadorned irony. That generations of people would choose to lean headlong into a frequently bleak, occasionally glorious, and outwardly unchanging landscape may seem baffling to those from more "exotic" or temperate places.

How can you explain that you "plugged your car in" so the engine block wouldn't freeze overnight? That you know from experience that you can run to the school bus every below-freezing morning with a wet head of hair and not die from consumption? That you drove a tractor at six, a pickup truck at ten, and got your first permit at 14? That you can change the oil, the tire, the battery, the spark plugs, build a birdhouse, a bookshelf, sew a pair of pants, embroider a pillowcase, knit a sweater, cook a four-course meal, field dress a deer—all of which you learned in school? That you understand completely why some people own guns, and that they aren't all dangerous, stockpiling, AK-47 toting militia men, even though you vividly remember that frigid February night in 1983 when US Marshall-murdering Gordon Kahl of Posse Comitatus was on the lam and your car was pulled over at a roadblock, and your trunk was searched?

We get it. We understand people who didn't grow up in this piece of heaven have questions, and we don't have easy answers, because we speak very little over a long cup of kitchen table coffee, only to spend twenty minutes saying goodbye in ice-plumed sentences beside a warming vehicle. Luckily, we do have prose and poetry, metaphor and irony. Read these pages and lean into the howling wind of a cold you will never forget.

-- Amy Scheibe is the author of the novel *A Fireproof Home for the Bride*.

One Winter Night

By Sadie Mendenhall-Cariveau

Vanessa rolled her eyes as she gripped the steering wheel. It had been years since she had been home. Still, it hadn't been quite long enough. She listened to her baby sister ramble on the phone about how irresponsible she was and something else about being inconsiderate of others.

"Look, I came back, didn't I?"

Their mother had passed away at the worst of times. It was something she didn't feel like explaining to her sister again. She listened to the sound of the tires on the grit spread on the road, sending the slush splashing dirtily onto the finger drifts of snow. It wasn't like winter up north was the only thing rough this time of year, but her rent was due and, in order to take the trip, she had to cancel a gallery opening that was supposed to pay that rent and her bills for the next month or so at least. Traveling alone was also no easy feat in scattered rain and snow showers either. It wasn't something she could hope to get her self-absorbed sister's pea brain to comprehend.

Vanessa took a deep breath, trying to remember to be mindful and find other means to cope with her sister. "I'm just saying that it sucks."

"How do you think I feel? I have a real job where I can't just pick and choose my hours. I have a husband who can't run off from his job whenever he wants, and we have three kids we have to be strong for. Let's not forget the holiday break vacation we planned that I'm probably going to have to cancel because you couldn't get up here sooner. Not like I didn't already cancel a scheduled luncheon with the girls, too, because somebody had to be present for the coroner."

There was a distinct clicking of a pen on the other side of the phone.

"Well, yeah, it was kind of your job to do that. You know, nearest living relative and all." Vanessa swore she heard her sister mumble something but decided not to bring it up. "Anyway, I'm here. I'm even pulling down the road as we speak."

"Good. I have to go. I'll try to be by after I get the kids down for bed tonight"

"Wait, what? You chewed me out and accused me of being selfish this whole time, and you aren't even here to greet me? Let alone help me, or I don't know, let me in?"

"It's not like I'm leaving you in a lurch. Cayden should be there already. He's been helping out with getting it all packed up."

"Seriously? You couldn't think of anyone else to meet me out here? Maybe one of your girls perhaps? Some random homeless person looking to make a quick buck?"

"I don't get what your deal is, Nessa. He's a good guy. He's not the Big Bad Wolf, and you're not Little Red Riding Hood. Grow up."

"Right, he's such a wonderful guy."

"Just chill, okay? It's been ages. You can't still be blaming him for something he had nothing to do with. Only God knows…"

"Yeah, sure." How could her sister be that naïve? She really had a lot of nerve. "Whatever, Ash, just get over here and help at your earliest convenience."

"Don't be that way, Nessa. Look, maybe while you're here you can come to-"

Vanessa hung up. She only wished that it could have been with an old school slam of the phone, or something with an audible click. She pressed her forehead to the steering wheel and took a deep breath, turned off the engine and grabbed the key fob. Here goes nothing, she thought as she grabbed her jacket from the passenger seat and opened the door. "Now here's a cold you can't forget." She grimaced as she rushed her arms into the warm fabric and shoved the fob into her pocket.

Light tufts of snow caressed her cheek as she made her way to the porch of her childhood home. The steps were shoveled and salted but showed clear signs of the abuse of the weather over the years. She looked over to the other end of the porch, shocked that the porch swing was still there. Her breath clung to the air when she chuckled. She was certain that were it not for the ice holding it together, the entire thing would splinter, taking with it the ghosts of her past as it crashed through the porch to the earth below. Perhaps it would free her of all the heartache –or at the very least make them bearable.

"Still a fan of black, I see." Cayden's midwestern drawl thrummed through her brain and reignited old grudges with its honeyed sound.

"Still Captain Obvious, I see." She tried to act playful, but her matter-of-fact tone dripped with sarcasm.

"Ouch, Ness. I was just trying to be polite." He held his arms open, a gesture that she understood was an invitation for a hug. "It's been a long time."

"Yeah, can we just go inside? It's a bit cold for my liking."

"I'm sure it is." He lowered his arms and stepped aside after opening the door. "After you."

"Mmm..." She moved by him, savoring the inviting warmth that greeted her when she crossed the threshold. One of her favorite things growing up was always the warmth indoors after a day of sledding and playing in the snow. She used to love hot chocolate by the fireplace, roasting marshmallows and staring into the flames.

"I tried to keep the house warm and get as much done as possible over the past several days to make it easier. I didn't touch anything in your mom's room, or anything that I remembered was far too sentimental for you girls."

"Hmm, us girls," she muttered, searching for the right words and trying not to sound curt. "If I didn't know any better, I'd think that you were more than just two years my senior. Where has Ashley been over these past several days? I was under the impression that she was the one getting the house packed up."

"Don't be that way, I offered to help out. You have to understand how rough it's been on all of us here, Ness."

"Vanessa. You'd think after growing up with me you'd know my name." She spun around, eyeing him. "And since when were you included in this us? I'm just trying to figure out your role here, so I know who and what this family is comprised of." The strident sound of her voice shocked her, but she didn't care.

"I've been here, Vanessa." There was added emphasis on her name this time. "You haven't. You left the first chance you got when Jackson died and you forgot to look back."

"Don't. Don't you dare bring my brother up." She closed the distance between them, glaring.

"Like it or not, it's true and you know it."

Vanessa felt the points of the equalizer on the fob in her palm. She had almost forgotten it was there. Even with her platformed boots on, she was still a foot shorter than Cayden. Being short was definitely a curse from where she was standing.

"I'm sorry." He hung his jacket up and held his hand out. "Let's just see what we can get done, alright?"

"Sure." She shrugged her jacket off and handed it to him, ashamed at how easily he had gotten under her skin. The last thing she wanted was to appear weak.

There was silence as they removed their boots. Once removed, they made their way through the foyer and up the four steps into the front room, Vanessa winced as she looked around. Stacks of boxes labeled Dishes, Towels, Craft Stuff, etc. were stacked as neatly as they could be in the bay window and along the wall in front of it. Traditionally, just after Thanksgiving, the tree would be there. Not this year.

She ran her hands over the couch and laughed. "I remember when Dad and Jackson fought to get this couch in here. The tight stairwell made it impossible, but Mom insisted it would fit. Jackson figured it out, always the pleaser."

"The logical one."

"He sure was. It was his idea to lift it up and over the banister. Mom was furious." She rubbed her thumb over a gouge that had darkened with age and years of Pledge and Old English being rubbed into the wood. They both stood there, silent for the moment.

It was Cayden's voice that intruded. "I left a few things in the kitchen, just a few cooking things, some paper and plastic ware. I wasn't sure how long you planned to stay, or if you'd want to eat out."

"I can't stay longer than a few days." She mustered a politeness she wasn't sure she had for him. "Thank you, though."

"Yeah, sure. It was nothing."

Vanessa walked off and headed down the hall, brushing her fingers along the wainscoting and wallpaper. Nothing to stop her now, no banshee wail about how she was going to ruin it or some other complaint. She paused at her mother's room, staring at the closed door.

When she was younger, there were times she had secretly wished for this day to arrive. Jackson had been her mother's favorite, with Ashley coming in a close second. Meanwhile, she had to suck it up and take whatever attention she could coax out; good, bad, it didn't matter. She took what she could get.

The day Jackson died her mother took to her room for months. She could still remember the putrid smell of cigarette smoke seeping under the door. It was the signal that her mother was awake. Next came the coughing and the whiney call for someone to bring her something to drink or eat. Ashley always jumped on it, eager to please as ever.

Vanessa softly rapped her knuckles on the door, knowing no one would answer. It was a silly thing, but it felt right. Upon entering, she squeezed her eyes shut, steeling her nerves as she crossed into the room. "Whelp, looks like it's finally time to dismantle your shrine, Mom."

She didn't look at the bed. Instead, she turned her back, flicked on the light and inspected the figurines, trinket boxes, and photos that graced the dresser top. Knowing that her mother died in this room softened her ever so slightly as she opened the drawers. One by one, she rifled through the clothing, noting what she did and didn't recognize as she set them on the floor. It didn't matter to her if the floor was clean or not. Her mother was dead, and the clothes were going to be donated. Besides, they all bore the same scent of cedar and nicotine, with undertones of something flowery.

How far she could reach in the dresser dictated her position. By the last drawer she was sitting cross legged. It was no surprise when she discovered the snapping boxes and tied bags holding her mother's favorite jewelry. She opened them, trying to remember the stories that accompanied them, but failed when she got to the uncovered bag. It was clear, zipped shut, and double sealed with red tape. Manilla folders showed through, Case File printed on the tabs. Beneath the files was the anticipated array of clothing her mother wore the day they learned of Jackson's death. The funeral pamphlet was tucked within the folds of a sweater, well-worn and spotted with stains from years of crying over it.

Vanessa sat silently rummaging through it all, pushing the world away. She almost missed the last bag, even though it was larger than the others. Evidence. She counted backwards, reminding herself that she was safe, secure and loved, over and over until she was sick of it failing. Coping wasn't her strong suit anyway.

"Fuck, Mom, why did you keep this?" It was obvious from the broken zipper on the bag and the traces of ashes inside that her mother had opened it more than once. Vanessa slammed it down atop the files, cascading the stack of jewelry boxes next to them onto the floor. "What in the absolute…"

"Hey, Ness? Did you need some of these boxes?" Cayden's heavy steps were coming closer.

"Yes, just bring a few and place them by the door." She sounded pitchy. "I'll let you know if I need more."

Within a few moments his footsteps softened. She sucked in air, grateful that the pain had eased. She hadn't noticed she was holding her breath until then. Standing up was a harder task than coping with what she had found. Tingles shot through her butt, legs, and feet as she made her way to the door.

Cayden handed her a couple of the boxes already neatly put together. "Did you need any help in here?"

"Nope, not unless you know how I can sit on the floor without my ass falling asleep, or a faster way of retrieving the feeling in my lower extremities."

"Well, now that you mention it…"

"That was rhetorical, idiot." She took the boxes and stomped off, shaking her head.

"Okay, then. Shout if you need anything."

"Yeah, yeah." he huffed as she shoveled the clothes forcefully into the boxes. She left the contents of the last drawer where it lay. She hadn't yet figured out how to pack that up for safe keeping. In reality, the room was nearly done. The closet had already been emptied for the most part before she arrived. All that remained was the vanity, and all the trinkets and photos that adorned the top of the dresser. Still, the heaviness remained.

She grabbed an empty box and placed it on the vanity chair. "Everything has its place. That's what you said, right Mother?" Vanessa traced in the dust, rubbing the grit between her fingers. If the dust wasn't a dead giveaway of how long everything had been in its place, the clean spot that appeared when she lifted the first decorative bottle was. She sniffed one of the bottles of perfume before stuffing it into her pocket. It was her favorite, and one she got her mother every year, even after she left home. The rest of the things she wrapped haphazardly with the brown paper and placed in the box. It was all she could do not to look up into the hazy mirror to the bed behind her, to seek out her mother's disapproval sitting against the pillows. She'd be palming her elbow to brace the trembling arm and shaky hand as she puffed away on her cigarette.

Soon as she started the vanity, she was done and moving away from the mirror. The tightness in her chest was back, listing everything she had hated about her mother, the things she held more precious than any of her children, the favoritisms. Worst still were the tears that Vanessa couldn't stop as she admitted what she loved about her mother. She braced herself on the dresser, pressing the flesh of her palms against the wood and trying to calm down. She let loose the sound of her agony as she straightened up and began flinging the little glass figurines of rabbits behind her towards the head of the bed.

"Damn you!" One by one she hurled them. The little rabbits in jackets, tutus and sweaters crashed against the wall where she imagined her mother. "Screw you! Screw you and all of your cotton-tailed fetishes! Screw your favoritism! Screw your disapproval of everything about me!" She threw an iridescent bunny holding a carrot basket against the headboard. "Why, Mother? Why wasn't I ever good enough for you?"

"Vanessa!" Cayden spilled through the doorway of the room, tripping on the pile of trinket boxes as he lumbered over to her. "Vanessa, what's wrong?" He placed his hand on her shoulder.

She clasped a little porcelain bunny cherub to her chest and slumped against the footboard. Cayden sat next to her.

"Feel better?"

She leaned against him when he placed his arm around her. "Maybe just a little." She held the statue in front of her, inspecting it. "Jackson used to get one for her every year. The rest of us just followed suit after he passed."

"I have to ask, why rabbits?"

"She loved Beatrix Potter. She would read us the tales every night before bed, every time we were sick. It was her thing to do when we were little."

"Sounds like some pretty good memories."

"We had lots of them when we were all together." She handed the bunny to Cayden, too exhausted to care about the grudge or anything. "Her first was a bunny family, one I probably smashed already. Dad got it for her the year Ashley was born. After that, he and Jackson would go hunting them out for all special occasions. When Dad died, Jackson continued to do it. This one, I got her. It was the first time I got one for her."

"Oh?" He handed it back to her.

"I got it for her after Jackson died. I hoped it would help her be her again."

"Nessa, I…"

"No, I know what you're going to say. You had nothing to do with his death. You weren't even with him." She nudged the bags with her toe.

"Your statement was the first one in the pile, the only one I recognized even with redactions."

"Spit it out. You know you want to, so just say it."

She straightened up and away from him. "Fine. Explain to me how, if you weren't with him, everyone else saw you leave with him? You told the police you weren't with him, and why? I believe you worded it as 'not liking how he was acting'?"

Cayden shook his head. "You weren't there. You can't understand how I was feeling that night. There were lots of things you didn't know, Ness."

"Then by all means, enlighten me."

He reached for the bags, opened the case file, and held it out to her. "Everyone had been drinking that night, it was a party. Summer was nearly over. School would be starting soon and it was our senior year."

"Yeah, I know. How could I forget? It was my brother that died, remember?"

"Jackson was supposed to be our DD. The responsible one."

"Duh, he never drank."

"Except when he did."

"No, he never…"

"Here's an idea, Miss Know-It-All, why don't you listen for a change."

She tightened her lips and gestured for him to continue.

"Your brother drank, and he drank a lot when it suited him. When it came right down to it, he preferred pills to drinking or, at the very least, mixing them together. That night, his cocktail of choice was oxy with an energy drink chaser followed by vodka. Uppers and downers were his weakness. If any of us called him on it, or tried to slow him down, he was nasty mean about it."

Cayden tapped on the tox screen. "Your mom was so disappointed when she found out. She made me swear to keep it secret from you, Ashley and anyone else that didn't know. That night he was doing double of everything to impress a college chic that was there. The more he popped, the more I was ready for us to leave before he ended up in the hospital."

"So what? You just decided to walk him onto the tracks halfway home?"

"You really are a bitch. Do you honestly think I could do that? He was my best friend, Nessa." He looked away from her. "I tried to get him to get in the cab with me, but he refused because of the pretty girl waiting by his car. I left him there, alive and feeling up on her. I had no idea he was going to drive her to the dorms, let alone that he would end up playing chicken with a damned train."

Vanessa sat, unblinking, trying to picture that side of her brother. Was Cayden telling her the truth or was he just tarnishing her memories to be cruel? She couldn't think straight. Looking at the report, listening to Cayden, she realized that perhaps there was a side she didn't know. She stood up and dropped the file on the floor between them.

"I'm going to head out." Her voice was alien even to her. She beelined for the front door with Cayden close behind her.

"Vanessa, you can't leave at this hour. It's below zero out there. You were on the road all day, up all night packing, you haven't eaten either. So just wait. Wait until later."

"No, I want to go."

"Do you not remember the snow out there?"

"What's your point?"

"Ness, please, the plows won't have been out yet. Wait until you've rested some and it's safe out there. You shouldn't be driving in the state you're in."

"Cayden, look, I appreciate your concern and your help, I do, but don't you have somewhere to be?"

"Yeah, I do." He came closer to her. "Right here, with you."

"You know what, screw this. Screw you, too. Mom and Ash may have fallen for that story of yours, but I'm not buying it. Accidents like that, someone driving around town just to play chicken with a train? That doesn't happen, Cayden. That's not something that people do. You don't just screw up like that. Jackson wouldn't have screwed up like that. The logical one, remember?" She shoved her feet into her boots and tucked the laces into the sides. "Someone is responsible for his death. He had to have been drugged. Jackson was always careful, always safe. He was the kid that mom wanted me to be like. He was my hero."

"You can try to run away all you want. Look for all the people in the world to blame. At the end of the day, you know I'm not lying." He thrust the reports into her hands. "You've read them. Look at the tox screen."

"It proves nothing, except that someone took advantage of him."

"No. It proves he was unstable. It proves he was on drugs and drinking. It proves that with the amount in his system he'd have thought he was unstoppable--if he wasn't hallucinating at that point."

She didn't bother putting her jacket on. She just grabbed it, took out her fob and stomped towards the door. "You know, it's hard to imagine that at one point in my life I actually liked you, that I believed I could trust you."

"You still can, Vanessa." He took her by the arm and pulled her closer. "You can still trust me." He wrapped his arms around her and hugged her close to his chest.

"Let me go, Cayden." She jerked free and ran outside. Her tears froze to her cheeks as she made it to her car. The temperature was much colder than she thought. She fought to get her jacket on and her car door open as he came up behind her.

"You just don't get it, do you?" She kept the door between the two of them, one foot inside. "He was my big brother. He was the golden child on the pedestal. The one with the bright future. I was just the failure that painted pictures and did stupid sculptures. I tried to be like him. I pushed myself as hard as I could, and still I wasn't good enough. I just kept failing."

"Your mother was so proud of you. Ashley is still jealous of you."

"See, you say things like that and I wish I could believe you, but I can't."

"Why not?"

"Because then I'm just the loser with a druggy for an idol."

"That's not true. You of all people know that everyone has more than one side. He struggled to keep his addictions hidden because of shame. He didn't want you knowing, your mom knowing. It was bad enough that I knew." He turned as though he was about to leave and let her go, but then he spun back around. "Was it really that much easier on you to think that I, his best friend, had killed him? That I was capable of that? Was it?"

"Nothing about any of this is easy, Cayden! Nothing! My dad is dead, my brother is dead, my mother is dead and all I'm left with is a sister who I don't really know because of a huge age gap. Hell, she hates me so much she didn't even bother to show up tonight. Instead, she stayed home with kids whose names and ages I mix up because I don't get updates unless I pry them off Facebook, and her husband who won't even add me on Facebook. I'm a ghost, and not just because I left, but because the only two people who saw me, or cared about me were dead. Why would I stay where I wasn't wanted?"

"I'm sorry I failed him. I should have tried harder to help him. I should have found a way to make him leave with me. I'm sorry I wasn't a better friend so that he would still be here for you." He placed his hand over hers on the door.

"Yeah, you should be." She pulled her hand away, got in her car and started it. She was grateful it started on the first try.

"You're seriously going to leave? It's after two in the morning, Ness."

"I need air. I need space, something, I don't know what. I just... I can't be here." She went to tug the door shut, but he held firm. "Cayden, please. I can't stay here cleaning up after a woman that told me what a mistake I was, for a sister that hates me just as much."

"She didn't tell you? She was never going to come tonight. She thought it would be easier on you if she waited 'til morning to come. She didn't want to fight with you tonight with it all being fresh for you."

"Is that so? Easier on me? Well, easier on me doesn't exist." She rubbed her hands against her cheeks.

"You aren't alone in this. I was here, and she will be here. Just come back inside where it's warm." Cayden stared at her, taking his hands off the door.

"I didn't ask for any of this."

"Nobody ever asks for this, but you can't just run away from it either."

"Watch me." She slammed her door shut and locked the car. She was glad he stepped back when he did as she put the car in reverse and did her best to speed off. Her wipers moved faster than her car seemed to, pushing the fresh powder from her windshield. She nearly veered off on ice when she left the drive and headed down the road. It wasn't as bad nearly as bad as she was afraid it would be, making it easier to get to a decent speed.

Cayden's headlights followed her in the rearview mirror. "Can't you take a hint?" She shook her head. "Damned idiot can't blame me if he ends up in a ditch." She turned up the heater and fiddled with the radio dial. When she glanced back up at the road, the eyes were the first thing she saw. Acting on instinct and fear, she slammed on the brakes. It was no use. The brake pedal was all the way down, but the car didn't slow, instead It kept lurching forward. She screamed on impact and the car spun out and into a ditch. The hood was buried in a snow drift, but the engine was still running. She tossed the car into reverse and tried to back up, but nothing happened.

Vanessa banged on the steering wheel, screaming loud enough that her throat hurt. She grabbed her phone from the floorboard and set it to flashlight mode. When she stepped out of the car, the cold sucked the breath from her, reminding her she had no gloves and that her boots were not made for the snow either. She cursed her wardrobe and slammed the door shut. "Figures, this would happen to me."

She scuttled up the side of the ditch and scanned the road. By the tracks, anyone else would think that more than one car went off the road tonight, but it was only hers. She looked around until she could see where they led and followed them. Nose hairs froze and flapped inside with every inhale and exhale like a caged bird beating its wings. It was one of the many pleasures of Minnesota winters and negative temperatures. Of course, like her dad used to say all the time, once it hits zero there's really not much else you can feel anyway.

She slowed when the clouds of condensation formed in time with the labored sounds of breathing. The light was dimmer than she wished and forced her to get closer in order to assess everything. At first, all she saw was the partially opened mouth, then the fear-stricken eyes. She froze. If asked, she couldn't say how long she stood there before headlights illuminated the scene, shrouding everything except the body before her in darkness.

"Vanessa, what the hell? Are you okay? Why are you stan…"

Cayden's voice was distant. She couldn't peel her eyes away from it all. His hands clasped her shoulders, and she could feel him tugging on her, trying to move her. Those eyes, those brown eyes bore into her.

Vanessa stepped back, numb to the cold that enveloped her. She could only watch as scarlet pooled in the snow. It spread thickly, like slow moving syrup on a snow-cone, melting parts of the ice as it moved.

"I had no choice. There was nothing I could…" She closed her eyes, shuddered, and hugged her jacket about her for warmth. She looked at the unusual position of the head and neck, the way the partially opened mouth and labored breathing had forced the tongue to skim the blood. "She was just there. First, there was nothing, no one. I just glanced down for a moment and when I looked up, there she was. I didn't have time to stop. I tried, but I couldn't. She was just standing there. I couldn't stop, and my car…"

Cayden pulled her into his arms and hugged her tightly. He rested his chin on the top of her head. "Nessa, it's okay. It's going to be okay."

"No, it won't. She's dying. She's suffering and she's dying and it's all my fault. I couldn't stop, and now she's going to die." Sobs wracked through her as she let him hold her.

"Come on, let's get you warm." He led her around to the passenger side of his truck. "I'll handle this. You just sit here and warm up." He reached over her lap and switched the heater on high, then grabbed his rifle from the rack on the back window. "Wait here, do you understand me?"

She nodded, pulled her knees to her chest, and sobbed. She heard him load the rifle, and she stared up at him. "Promise me it will be fast, that she won't have to suffer anymore?"

"I promise, Vanessa. She won't suffer. I'll make it quick."

When the door shut moments later, she tightened her arms around her knees. She watched him walk in front of the truck, blocking her view of the body. She squinted her eyes as tight as she could and bawled loudly into her knees. A single shot pierced the night causing her to jump.

"I'm so sorry," she whispered.

The driver's side opened a few minutes later. Cayden hung the rifle on its rack and slid into the truck.

"What happens now?" She looked sideways at him and watched as he ran his fingers through his hair.

"Now? Now I get my hunting license out and we wait." He closed the door before reaching over and pulling an envelope out of the glove box. "The police will likely be here first, followed by DNR to confirm everything and examine the doe. They'll make a decision and we'll go."

"That's it?"

"That's it." He sighed. "Well, no that's not it. Look, Vanessa, accidents happen all the time. Everywhere. It's that simple. Sometimes, it's no big deal, other times they're pretty shitty. Hell, look at tonight. You're from here, damn it. You know how these parts get, especially at night and especially in the winter. This was your accident, just like your brother's was his."

Fresh sobs poured from her. "I'm sorry, I'm so sorry, Cayden."

"Jesus Christ, come here." He wrapped his arms around her, this time running his hands through her hair. "I didn't mean to make you cry. Again."

"I'm just so sorry. I blamed you for so long. I didn't want to believe you. I didn't want Jackson to be gone. I needed something to hold on to. I know accidents happen. I'm not an idiot." She couldn't stop the tears from falling. She scooted closer to him and clung to him as she broke. She broke about everyone and everything, from her dad all the way up to the doe.

When she finally stopped crying, she turned and looked out the window. The doe was no longer staring but was covered in a thin blanket of white. The snow had all but erased the tracks, leaving the blood a soft pink. The blue morning light made everything seem peaceful. She had forgotten the melancholy beauty of Minnesota in the winter.

-- Since she was a child, Sadie Mendenhall-Cariveau has had a passion for writing and remembers telling teachers and family members that she wanted to be a writer. She has won awards, certificates and scholarships for her essays, short stories and poetry since sixth grade. Sadie became more inspired and determined to see her dreams come to fruition while serving in the United States Air Force and began participating in workshops and pursuing degrees in Creative Writing. Drawing inspiration from her own life and everything she feels affected by, her writing has been published in both online and in-print journals. Her goal is to complete her poetry collection and her book and to never stop writing.

The Universal Tree

By Barbara Bustamante

During the winter of 1969 in Minneapolis, Minnesota, six female university students shared expenses by renting a house together and sharing the boundaries that came with it.

Sharon shared a bedroom with Linda. Sharon, studying education, was an outspoken city girl and made her Norwegian heritage apparent. Linda, studying nursing, was from a small town and enjoyed all the stories provided by the "know-it-all" Sharon.

Suzy, a new college freshman, was a petite woman at the height of 4'11". She had a boyfriend, David, and all the women were eagerly waiting for him to pop the question. Suzy shared a bedroom with Terri, an older student from Eastern Europe who was studying medicine.

Jean and Donna occupied the two smaller bedrooms in the basement. Jean, a tall woman from the country, was studying home economics and enjoyed her German culture. Donna, studying English literature, had grown up in a small city in Wisconsin.

After dinner one evening before Thanksgiving, Linda curiously asked, "What is everyone doing for Christmas? I mean, are we having any parties, giving presents to each other, and having a tree?

All six began talking at once until suddenly Sharon raised her voice, "Well, parties and gifts are just fine, but we have to have a tree."

"Of course, we need a tree right *after* Thanksgiving," Linda chimed in.

"Why so early? The middle of December is perfect," countered Donna.

"Well, my family has always trimmed the tree the week before Christmas," added Jean.

Suzy glanced at Sharon and said, "I don't care when we get a tree, just so it's pretty."

"It's final! We'll pick up a tree from a tree lot on Friday," declared Sharon.

Terri shook her head, "How is this going to work out with me celebrating Eastern Orthodox Christmas in January?"

"A tree from a tree lot will never last until January and besides, I'm allergic to the preservatives on cut trees," Jean informed them.

In search of a solution, Donna scanned the phone book. "Look what I found, a tree farm on the other side of St. Paul."

"That sounds great," Terri replied, "as long as the tree will last until January 7th."

"Of course, it will last and it will be freshly cut with a real natural pine scent."

Eventually, they decided to get it from a tree farm. Since none of the women had a car, Suzy offered to ask David to drive his car. Jean and Donna volunteered to go along with Suzy and David to help pick out the perfect tree. Meanwhile, Terri, Sharon, and Linda would stay home to move furniture and unpack the Christmas decorations.

So, with a plan in place, they headed out the day after Thanksgiving to get their Christmas tree. The freeway through south Minneapolis and into St. Paul was a bit of a drive. Jean had written down the directions to the tree farm since they didn't have a map. They knew they were getting close to their destination when the scenery changed from urban to rural. Several twists and turns in the road later, they finally arrived at the farm. After carefully parking the car, they all received instructions, and started the trek through the rows of trees.

Each of them perused different types of trees and found one that suited their liking. Donna picked out a Fraser Fir, Jean chose a Scotch Pine, and David found a beautiful White Spruce, but based on the height, shape, and fullness, they unanimously agreed on the Balsam Fir selected by Suzy. Once they had the tree cut, loaded onto their car, and paid for, they set off to bring their precious cargo home.

Excitement built as they arrived home and unloaded, set up, and trimmed the tree. When all the tree lights were turned on, everyone was so very proud of this gorgeous Christmas tree that they celebrated their united effort.

Initially using a calendar, each woman signed up for seven days of tree watering duty. At first, caring for the tree was effortless. Each woman took her turn ensuring that the base of the tree was thoroughly watered each morning and night. As Christmas Day inched closer, attention to the tree began to waver, requiring repeated reminders to water the tree.

"Linda, how can you leave for Christmas break on Friday when you've also signed up for tree watering the same day?" Donna reminded her.

"Oh, shoot!" Linda grumbled. "Do you think Terri will switch days since she will be here over Christmas?"

During Christmas break, some of the women went home to be with their families. Terri and Suzy remained in the house, caring for the tree. By Christmas Day, not one needle had fallen from the tree—according to those who vacuumed the carpet.

Linda returned first from the holiday. After unpacking she commented, "It's too bad we can't throw out the tree. I have some great ideas for decorating for New Year's Eve."

Terri countered, "Don't get too anxious to get rid of the tree. We have an agreement to take care of it until I celebrate the Nativity on January 7th. The calendar is still here and it's your turn in a couple of days."

So the practice of reminding each other of their responsibility to keep the base of the tree watered continued.

At bedtime one night, Jean turned out her light and hollered to Donna in the bedroom next to hers, "Did you remember to water the tree tonight?" She then heard the pitter-patter of feet climbing the stairs to and from the kitchen to water the tree.

Another time Sharon reminded Linda by leaving a message for her on the light switch when she got home from a late date.

By New Year's Day Terri's holiday was only a week away. One evening as she entered the house, Suzy remarked, "Our tree still looks just as nice as when the lights were first switched on."

Linda took a second look at the tree. "It's amazing how long the tree has lasted without dropping a needle."

"I didn't think we would make it. Every other tree that I've had would have dried out by now," added Donna.

Terri joined in. "There's only a few more days left. I'm so grateful and proud of all of you for helping out. Since we started on November 28, we have nurtured this tree by checking the water level every morning and night. Thank you so much. This means a lot to me."

On Thursday, January 7th, Terry got ready for church and the rest of the women headed out for morning classes. Terry was so proud of the tree that she took a picture for her photo album. Her day would be filled with celebration and a small dinner with friends from church. At bedtime that evening, she noticed a single dried needle on the skirt under the tree.

She quietly thanked God for the wonderful gift that had united their household. And she turned off the light.

--Barbara Bustamante holds a BUS Degree in Food and Nutrition from North Dakota State University. She is semi-retired and lives in Moorhead, MN with her cat.

This Story Has No Title

By Rick Bylina

The song goes, "Oh, the weather outside is frightful...," and it is. And I know better than to start off a story with the weather, but in this case, it's appropriate. Mother Nature's weather is acting like a full-grown, petulant child. It is a character, bending the pine trees in the howling wind like a synchronized exercise class of nubile adolescent girls—touch those roots. The snow swirls, white-outs the scenery, and then settles in a quiet spot, mounding like the overflowing basket of whites that needs to be washed. The cold outside stings exposed skin like tiny ant bites. And when it invades the house, it seeps into my bones and makes getting up to go to the bathroom raise memories of the ache inside my muscles from last year's flu. They are too cold to stretch but respond dramatically when my butt touches the frost-bitten toilet seat.

The weather outside commands me to lay a sheet, four blankets, and two quilts on my bed. I crawl beneath it all for a nap and feel smothered, as though I'm losing a wrestling match with Hulk Hogan and he is on top, pinning me without mercy.

"Let me breathe."

"Oh, the weather outside is frightful…" I try to remain positive as I lie in bed unable to nap, one quilt removed, and Hulk Hogan banished to his corner. The single-digit temperatures and continuing snowfall are positive aspects of the changing of the seasons even if at the moment the house rocks in a near-hurricane gust of wind. Seventy-four miles per hour is the requirement for a hurricane. Is it possible that's what is happening as the storm bombs-out off the east coast of North Carolina like Godzilla approaching Tokyo with evil intent?

Mosquitoes. Yes. As the storm drives a steep ski slope of snow up the side of the house, I realize mosquitoes are having a tougher time than I. Yes, some will somehow survive—I don't get how—yet this cold should diminish their numbers. Tulips. Yes. The fragrant, ever-popular flower needs the cold to regenerate. In fact, all the bulbous members of the tulip family need the cold. And the blue spruces, lilacs, and several other flowers that strut their stuff up north, but struggle in the south, they all need winter's bite. Bring it on! Oh wait, don't bring it on too much. I have some bushes that don't like this visit from the polar vortex.

I don't want to, but I rise from the bed still thinking of the snow in positive terms. Snowflakes trap dissolved organic nitrogen, nitrate, ammonium in the atmosphere and deliver it free-of-charge to cold and quiet fields. With its warmer brother rain, they provide two-to-twenty-two pounds of much-needed nitrogen per acre each year. A layer of snow also insulates the soil, giving winter crops moisture to absorb. This layer of white can raise the temperature of the soil a few degrees. Winter wheat bows in appreciation, or maybe from another gust of wind.

I don't bow, I cringe, when I open the door to throw out another round of seeds to the birds. Black- and Brown-capped chickadees, countless sparrows, several types of woodpeckers, and hundreds of goldfinches, purple finches, and house finches don't wait until I close the door to forage. In a few minutes, I return with the tea kettle and boiling water to dissolve the ice in the gurgling water fountain. It is the only source of running water in the area. And once inside, bird squabbles subside as cardinals, Carolina wrens, blackbirds, and mourning doves crowd the watering hole for a drink. It's December. Everyone, including the birds, knows that snow is not ripe until January.

"Oh, the weather outside is frightful…" With the birds fed, I need to replenish the wood stove. Fortunately, I've gotten smarter over the years. I have a wheelbarrow full of wood in the garage, saving me from trudging outside to the shed to get a load. I flick on the light in the garage, and ten seconds later, the power goes out. "Good thing I heat with wood," I tell the mice who I know live in hidden spots in my disheveled garage. It's cold in the garage, but forty-seven degrees seems toasty when measured against the single digits outside. The mice are grateful that I am sloppy when filling up my birdseed bucket. I remind them, "Don't go into the house."

The power outage will last a few days, I suspect. With this wind and the mounting snow, I pity the on-call repairmen. I reload the fire doing my best Tom Hanks impression from "Castaway", "Me. I have made fire." Then it's time to light the candles already in place. When you're the third to last house on the electrical grid, you get used to being prepared for losing power in a storm. Anything that happens up-the-line affects us down-the-line, and I am the third to last house on the line. I call in the outage and discover that I'm the fourth one to report it. "There are twenty-seven outage zones and 312,000 people out of power. You are the twenty-sixth zone. We will address your issue by Tuesday at 11 a.m." It's Saturday now. Power outages get repaired in the order in which they reported, but the prioritization is by the number of people affected in the zone. I wonder who are the poor people in the twenty-seventh outage zone. The automated power company AI says, "There are sixteen people affected in your zone." There are twelve of us on our exurbia wooded outpost. Fortunately, the power company uses the Disney approach to time estimates. The Tuesday time will be adjusted to Monday night, and we will praise the power company.

A squirrel flies by the window.

I think about that an hour later as the last vestiges of sunlight depart, and it's me and a dozen candles listening to the wind howl. The only logical explanation for the squirrel was a dropped dinner by a hawk or owl who live in the woods surrounding me. My yard is a buffet for them with all the birds I feed, and the freeloader squirrels by the dozens just hanging around, scratching, eating, drinking, having sex, jumping into bushes for no reason, and just acting, squirrelly. The birds have departed for their hidden nesting sites.

The wind dies down. From severe gusts to nearly nothing in ten minutes as if the sun dragged the ferocious winds with it over the horizon. The snow appears to have slackened, but the wind blows so hard, I'm not sure. The quiet of the surrounding woods was nature at its best for about thirty minutes. Then, the chorus of generators coughed to life, and I search for my flashlight.

I dress like Nanook of the North, and deep-down inside me, I realize that fewer and fewer people over the years know what that means or have seen the 1922 documentary about life in the Arctic. I step outside, and I'm transported there with Nanook and his family, chewing on whale blubber and skinning snow rabbits. A foot of snow is difficult in most places. Nanook would laugh at it and use one of the thirty-seven words in the Inuit language to describe it—probably something that translates into 'puny powder' or, as I step through the snow, "muruaneq," meaning soft deep snow. In the Carolinas, it is a modern-day Armageddon.

The smell of pine permeates the air, and I see several twenty-footers laying on their sides at the edge of the forest. Fortunately, they aren't blocking anything and haven't fallen on something important—like my house. The cold pinches my nostrils. From then on, I'm a mouth breather. A perfect natural funnel has drifted the snow six-feet-high, stopping just to the bottom lip of the bedroom window. Ten feet away is bare ground is exposed, and six crazy daffodil bulb stems poke about a half-an-inch out of the soil. They will survive. I planted these bulbs in a spot that gets the most sun all winter and are visible reminders from my window that Spring is inevitable. I turn off the flashlight.

The clouds have departed; stars dominate the sky. However, I can see the spot on the horizon where the moon is inching its lordly self upward into the heavens. Despite my chattering teeth, I'm rewarded with six shooting stars (okay, meteorites) in the ten minutes I can stand to be outside. It is starkly beautiful—a black and white portrait. It is about eight degrees—record territory. In four days, the temperature will rise to the upper 60s. Welcome to the South.

"Oh, the weather outside is frightful..." It's a comfortable 65 degrees in the main room. I have chocolate, food, water, a book, candles, toilet paper, milk, and bread--all the essentials. "...And the fire's so delightful..."

--Rick Bylina lives with his wife near Apex, NC on five-wooded acres full of writing inspiration. Is that Big Foot? Ongoing corporate downsizing in the early 2000s convinced him to tap into his passion. He scribbled any crazy idea that crossed his mind. After gaining discipline, he wrote his debut novel, *One Promise Too Many*, to modest success. Though he likes writing mystery novels, he has published a book of poetry, a collection of short stories, and a memoir.

The Island

By William R. Bartlett

He stood on the snow-covered island, gazing at the ice that surrounded them. "Do you have to go?"

She took a deep breath. "This is wonderful! I feel like I can see forever."

The snow covering the trees vanished.

"You didn't answer my question."

"I didn't think I needed to."

He kicked some snow onto the ice, even though he wore only light sandals. "I'd rather you stayed."

"Do we have to go through this again?"

He said nothing.

She squinted at the snow-covered bridge that led from the island to the opposite shore, not much more than a stone's throw away. "You know I'll come back. I always do." The snow on the bridge disappeared, much like the snow on the tree limbs had, mere seconds before.

"So far. How do I know you will this time?"

"Oh, don't be such a baby. Where's your faith?"

"I just don't like being away from you." He stooped and brushed snow from the ground until he found a small, disc-shaped rock, about the size of his palm, and nestled it into his forefinger. Knees bent, he threw the stone onto the ice, sidearm as if he was trying to skip it across water. The little rock bounced and clattered as it slid along the frozen lake. "You said that's one of the things you love about me."

"I wasn't lying. Even after all these years, I love you more than ever."

"Then, don't leave. Let's go back home. We can sit on the terrace and eat Kalamata olives stuffed with herbed feta while we drink retsina. There's no reason to wait for the holiday. You being at home would make it special enough. We can even have pomegranates for dessert."

She gave him a steady look. "You're being ridiculous, and you know it." The snow on the ground dissipated, leaving the grass brown and flattened with no trace of moisture. "Why'd you bother coming to see me off if you're going to be like that? Why didn't you just stay home?"

He turned away from her and stared toward the trees on the distant shore, dim and misty in the morning fog. "I wanted to spend as much time with you as I could. You don't know what it's like when you're gone."

"Of course not, you goose." She laughed and stepped through the dried underbrush until she stood next to him. None of the bushes shook or quivered from her passage. "How could I?" The ice covering the lake turned to liquid, and the rock he'd thrown slid below the surface, leaving not so much as a bubble to mark its sinking.

"You know what I mean." He put his arm around her shoulders. "I only wish..."

She stepped in front of him, wrapped her arms around his back, and pulled herself tight, her head against his chest. "It's nice being with you, too. I'll be back before you know it. Besides, I still think you're hot."

"That's no comfort." He lowered his face and kissed her. "Promise me you'll return."

"Of course, I will. I always have." She kissed him again. "Nothing I could possibly imagine would keep me away." She squeezed him, fast and hard, then stepped out of his arms. "You'd better get going. The fog will lift soon, and you know how that affects you. Don't forget, you still have a kingdom to run."

"I suppose you're right."

"And give me a smile. Don't you want me to remember the charmer I met all those years ago?"

"If you really want to see a happy face, picture me when you're home again." He raised the corners of his mouth, but the smile didn't extend to his eyes.

"That's better. We'll be on the terrace together so fast, you'll wonder where the time has gone." She glanced toward the sun, a sliver visible through the bare trees, tiptoeing up past the horizon. "You should hurry. It's almost time."

The smile dropped from his face and he held his hand out at arm's length, palm down. Without a sound, a deep hole opened below his feet, expanding until it was wide enough for both of them. He descended into the hole as though being lowered by a crane and was soon lost in the darkness.

The ground closed as quietly as it had opened, until only a solid piece of earth remained, but his voice came out of the soil around her. "Goodbye, Persephone."

A fond smile lightened her expression. "Goodbye, Hades."

--William R. Bartlett is retired from the insurance industry and currently writes the *Word from Dad* feature in Kansas City Parent magazine, which he's done since the April 2009 issue. A lifelong resident of the Kansas City area and no stranger to snow, he's currently putting the finishing touches on a romance novel, *Nude, Light Housekeeping*.

The Hunt
By T.J. Fier

I was born under the bitter winter sun on the coldest night of the season. I'm sure a flicker of disappointment crossed both my mother's and father's faces when they first looked between my legs. Their fourth girl in as many years. They had prayed to the gods for a strapping boy and got me instead. Even worse, their prayers were half answered, for the moment I realized the difference between girls and boys, I knew I wasn't like either one.

Unlike my thoughtful sisters who mirrored my mother in all tasks, I initially took more interest in my father's daily labors. Most of the village boys helped their father with caring for livestock, mending fences, and hunting game, and without a son, my father appreciated my extra pair of hands. Much like him, I couldn't stand the confines of home and came alive when outdoors. But eventually my mother bore sons. Once they grew old enough, I would be sent to my expected place at her side.

My father did not hesitate to remind me of this eventuality: "You are a great help, Mara. Yet, you still must learn to be more like your sisters."

I couldn't stand cooking, helping care for my younger siblings, or scrubbing floors, but found enjoyment in my mother's loom and spinning wheel. Weaving, much like hunting, was one of the few tasks that quieted my restless mind. While I spun wool or created an intricate pattern on the loom, I tried to weave my future. Who would I become as an adult? Could I make my own way, or would I become a wife and mother like most women in our village? The way never made itself clear. I often dreamt myself tall, broad, and strong as many of the men in our village, with a woman much like my mother at my side. These visions only added to my confusion.

Searching for greater truth, I turned to our gods.

We prayed to many local deities in our village. Our patron god Goare was a harsh, gruff man of the hunt. According to our lore, he wed Metis, the fertile goddess of the hearth before the time of man. To honor our god, our men strove to be accomplished hunters, protectors, and providers. The womenfolk emulated Metis by caring for the home and producing as many children as possible.

But I felt unseen by the gods, for I could not connect to either. I turned to our sacred books, scouring them for an answer. There, I found a possible patron in the trickster god, Eliki, sibling of Goare. They—for Eliki was neither man nor woman but both—traveled the world below, above us, and in between. A creature who moved among all worlds. This was what I wanted: freedom to be and do as I pleased.

I told no one of my new devotion and prayed to Goare to forgive me for picking his lesser sibling to worship instead of him. If Goare was offended, he never let it be known. If Eliki accepted me as their supplicant, they did not acknowledge me either.

Using my skills as a weaver and hunter, I wove dried grass and wheat into a crown worthy of a god. I hunted and killed a beautiful rooster pheasant. Then, building a fire, I burned them both as an offering to Eliki. I cried out to them in the woods when no one else could hear. I even chose a new name, a proper name for the person I ought to be. I was born Mara, but someday I would become Mox. I told Eliki my name, for names held power. Eliki gave no sign of hearing my prayers, but I refused to give up. I was getting older and, in time, my body would decide my path.

By my thirteenth winter, I could shoot an arrow straight as any lad, ride a horse bareback, and strip the hide from a hare in one swift yank. My skills as a weaver were known throughout the village, which, according to my mother, would help fetch me an excellent bride price. I did not want to be anyone's bride. There was only one boy in the village, Gren, who might treat me with some kindness and understanding. I had great affection for the strapping, red-cheeked boy, but he had been promised to the Head Elder's daughter several years before.

When we attended our weekly worship, no matter how much I cried and raged, my mother shoved me into dresses and put flowers in my braided hair. One summer solstice, I whipped off my skirt right before our whole village and revealed a pair of altered breeches stolen from my father's wardrobe. He thrashed me with a violence that frightened even him.

"We cannot go on like this," he whispered at my bedside while I recovered. Tears glossed his eyes despite the determined set to his jaw. "You bring dishonor to our family. You don't hear how they speak of you in the village. You could cause your sisters' suitors to run off. You must act appropriately."

I said nothing, for I would not make unfaithful promises.

Instead, I pretended to heed my father's words as my bruises healed. I helped Mother more but stole outside at every opportunity, even when another harsh winter descended from the mountains and settled into our valley. The cold never bothered me, for I was a child of the winter. And in the winter, I could hide my developing body beneath layer after layer and pretend I wasn't becoming a woman.

Once, after Father chided me for shirking my household duties, I told him, in a fit of desperation, that I was like Eliki. He looked at me as if I had grown horns.

"For shame," he said, his crooked smile twisting into a frown. "In this village, we honor Goare and Metis and none other. You must do the same. The Trickster has no place here, and you should not look upon such a devious creature for salvation."

I knew better than to argue or to bring up Eliki again. But in my heart of hearts, I refused to give up. For if a god could not save me, then no one could.

Each morning before anyone else rose, I wrapped a long bandage around my chest, praying this would stave off the inevitable. I continued to braid my hair and used my mending skills to take out the seams on my one pair of breeches. They were growing increasingly tight, and I knew Mother would not sew me another pair.

Desperate, I prayed to Eliki with growing fervor. I scoured our sacred texts for anything that might help me. Eliki made only rare appearances in our books. Often, they popped in to cause a little trouble before disappearing into the woods again. They took on the guise of men, women, children, and even the occasional animal when sowing a little bit of chaos. However, what looked like mischief, often turned out to be a bit of good in disguise.

According to one story, summer used to never end--until Eliki stole the blanket off a sleeping Goare. This caused Goare to freeze, bringing on the very first winter. Our patron god was only revived when Metis found him and gave her love a life-restoring kiss, which brought the world back to life. And so began our yearly cycle of seasons.

I didn't seek to cause trouble or sow discord. My cleverness lay in my actions. Using every length of spare yarn I could find, I stayed up late by candlelight for over a month to weave a blanket worthy of a god's attention. And I had a specific pattern in mind. Once upon a time, Eliki had taken on the mantle of a bear to frighten Goare and I did my best to recreate the scene of Eliki the bear chasing his scared brother up a tree.

My blanket was more of a shawl when done, but my careful workmanship made it a worthy gift. According to legend, Eliki had an affinity for oak trees, so I left my offering in the deepest part of the woods on the lowest branch of an ancient one, praying Eliki would accept it. I swore one more time to do whatever it took for me to become more like Eliki. And I meant it. Anything.

The winter of my fourteenth year was unlike the others. On my name day, snow fell in shorn curtains, blown wildly about by a wind wailing like an evil spirit. Within a few days, snow had piled up to my waist, nearly burying several cattle and suffocating the neighbor's sheep. I helped my father shovel snow from neighbors' roofs and clear paths between buildings. While my little brothers complained of aching backs and frozen feet, I reveled in the physical activity. So many of the villagers were grateful for my help, they forgot to give me their cold, sidelong glances. Such moments gave me hope, but it only took one of the neighbor boys laughing at my breeches for me to lose confidence.

That first blizzard was only the beginning. More storms came with the same wailing wind and bitter temperatures. The snow piled up to the eves. Chickens froze in their nests. A man went missing when he attempted to feed his hungry cattle in the middle of one storm. We knew his body wouldn't be found until spring.

Some began to whisper about this winter being cursed. Did we not make the proper sacrifices to Metis so she would again bring the spring? Did our appeals to Goare to protect our livestock during the winter months fall flat? We were certain the gods must've been displeased with us. As more villagers grew desperate, muttering began that I, the strange girl who acted too much like a boy, was the cause of our suffering. The dark looks returned. In desperation, I went into the woods to hunt for whatever game I could find. Fresh meat tended to quiet angry, hungry hearts.

It worked…for a little while. But soon the small rabbits and grouse were depleted. We needed game meat or we would starve.

Father arranged the annual midwinter hunt despite the forbidding weather. Several men didn't join due to exhaustion. I could sense Father's dismay at the lower numbers. Women were not permitted on the hunt and yet, Father handed me my bow and told me to "bundle up."

"Your skills with the bow are needed, Mara," Father said as I counted my arrows. "But when the spring returns, you will teach your brothers all you know, and they will take over hunting duties. Then you will stay with your sisters to care for hearth and home. I still believe that you can become a woman Metis would admire."

I bit back my response. I would never give up on my dream to run free, not even if they attempted to bind me to a man beyond my father.

The hunt started at dawn. Our party included my father, three other village men, two elder sons, and me, drifting like a shadow behind them all. I sensed the men's displeasure at my presence, but they didn't say a word.

As we headed out, Gren gave me a smile and a nod. My heart ached for a moment, but the feeling soon passed when he smacked my shoulder, nearly sending me into a snowbank. "I care not what others say. You're the best shot in the village."

I blushed and didn't say a word, silently mourning the loss of something that could never be. As I followed in his wake, appreciating the wide spread of his shoulders, I envied everything about him, including his future.

We moved in single-file until we reached the depths of the forest where the trees shielded the ground from the thickest snow-cover. We broke into two groups. I joined my father and Gren. The three of us trekked up the nearest ridge to get a better view of possible quarry. The rest would move in a line through the valley, hoping to flush out anything hidden among the snow-crusted bramble.

Using the path cleared by Father and Gren, I crept up the ridge. An uneasy feeling settled in my bones. Usually, when the air bit my cheeks as it did that morning, the sky above cleared to welcome a brilliant sun haloed by a ring of glimmering ice. Instead, dark clouds covered the sky and grew heavier the deeper we crept into the woods. The sky reminded me of a bruise, undulating between purple, blue, and the occasional yellow.

"I haven't seen such a sky since I was your age, Gren," Father said.

"There is a weight to the heavens," Gren whispered, as if afraid someone or something beyond our small group would hear him. "Could this be an enchantment?"

"It was last time." My father shifted his longbow and turned back to me. "I swore I saw the Death God's minions walking among us like shadow made flesh. Be wary, my child. Unholy creatures may be afoot."

"Look," I said, pointing to a set of tracks cutting through the valley below. "Why would a bear come out in the winter?"

"I knew this season was cursed." Father bowed his head, pressing his fingers to his forehead, lips, then chest. "Goare protect us. If you see this beast, whatever you do, don't run. And don't make eye contact. If you try to shoot it down, you'll only anger the bear. Back away slowly until he loses interest."

"And if he charges?" Gren surveyed the trees with worried eyes.

Father scraped away the ice clinging to his shaggy beard. "Stand your ground. You cannot outrun a bear. Come, keep an eye out below for quarry. I pray that Goare heeds our desperation and sends fresh meat our way."

We each took a position overlooking the clearing below. From where I sat, I could see both my father and Gren hidden among the boulders a stone's throw away. If we were lucky in our hunt, we would soon turn the snow from white to red.

Instead of growing warmer and brighter as the day grew old, the heavens thickened and swirled, full of the strange, bruised clouds. Soon light snow fell, the flakes like goose down tumbling from the sky. I stuck out my tongue and caught the clotted ice. Their flavor was strange, almost sweet, like honey.

I turned to see if my father also noticed the strange nature of the snow, but the flurries created a hazy screen between us. Hunting would be impossible in such weather.

I considered heading his way when a great exhale of breath echoed along the base of the valley. At first, the sound was a voice on a breeze, whispering in an unknown language. The whisper grew into a huffing noise, like a man gasping for breath. The gasps grew in length and depth, gathering into one incredible, throbbing roar until they shook the rocks beneath me.

"A bear," I cried, fighting to see anything through the snow.

A disembodied voice murmured upon the wind. *You forgot that blood is always required for a proper sacrifice.*

I stood, searching for the person who spoke the cryptic words. Did anyone else hear them? Or just me?

Like a curtain dropping from the clouds, the snow immediately ceased. Shouts echoed below. The rest of our hunting party scrambled beyond the tree line, fighting their way through the snowbanks. They kept looking over their shoulders, eyes turned in horror to what pursued them.

A massive white beast crashed through the trees. An albino bear, twice the size of a normal one, took down a man so fast the hunter didn't have time to scream. Blood spattered across blinding white snow. The bear shook the hunter like a rag doll, ripping open his screaming throat.

"You can't outrun a bear! Climb high as you can!" Father screamed, waving his arms to get the others' attention. "And don't let go, whatever you do. Don't let go!"

The other hunters took advantage of their friend's demise, quickly climbing up trees too small for such a massive bear to scale. The men climbed high as they dared and cried out in horror as the bear tested their perches one by one. The beast, nearly as tall as our house, shook each tree, ripping away low-hanging branches. The hunters held tight.

"Bears can't climb rocks, can they?" Gren shouted as he scrambled along the slick stone toward where my father crouched.

The strange voice whispered, *Shall I take them too?*

The bear, red dripping from its great maw, raised its head toward my screaming father. The beast shook its massive head and charged, easily scaling the snowdrifts piled high along the base of our ridge. It reared up, terrible paws scratching at the stone.

"This is no ordinary bear." Father stepped back, surveying the rocks further up the hill. "Let's get higher. Mara, climb as high as you can. There must be another way down on the other side of the ridge.

The hillside was easy to scale for Father's and Gren's large bodies and long limbs. I surveyed the surrounding rocks but was met by sheer rock faces each way I turned, no handhold or a foothold in sight. Below, the bear let out another gut-churning bellow, its mighty voice shaking my bones.

I have come for you, little one.

"C'mon Mara, hurry," Father cried when he realized I hadn't followed them.

I turned in circles, scraping away snow, searching for somewhere, anywhere, to find purchase and pull my body up the rocks.

The bear, despite its bulk, scaled the steep hillside and headed right for me. Crimson-stained paws pushed him higher and higher.

There had to be a way out. I scanned the path I had taken to get to my perch, but it led directly to the bear. If I followed the path my father had taken to get to his—

Mox, do not run.

I shuddered, searching the sky for my invisible tormenter. How could a spirit know my chosen name? I had whispered the name into the wind a thousand times, but I had never received any sign of having been heard.

You finally brought me a worthy offering, and I have come to answer your prayers.

I turned to discover two bright, intelligent eyes in the face of the ravenous white beast. The bear had crept closer to me than I realized. I could smell the hot iron scent of blood on its huffing breath.

"Mara!" My father screamed, true terror in his voice. "Climb, you have to climb!"

Do not listen to someone who never truly appreciated you for who you are.

The bear seemed to glare at my father who, in his desperation, nocked an arrow and sent it flying toward the bear. The bear easily dodged the projectile, a growl rumbling deep in its great throat.

"Who are you?" I whispered.

You know me. You've called to me for years, my child. Now that you have finally given me proper tribute, I am willing to bargain.

In my terror, I hadn't noticed the odd scrap of fabric tangledinto the bear's white fur. I recognized the blanket I had woven by candlelight as an offering to my chosen god.

"Eliki?" I nearly fell to my knees. "You heard me? Why did you not come before now?"

The bear licked its gore-thick maw. *I told you, Mox. You read my stories. Did you not remember that all promises must be sealed with blood? What you ask for requires a great sacrifice.*

My father's entreaties faded into the background.

I can give you what you desire, Mox. I can make you like me.

My breath caught in my throat. "You can stop me from becoming a woman?"

Of course. I am Eliki, after all.

"What must I do?" Gazing into the eyes of a god, even in a different form, proved difficult. The bear seemed to see into my soul.

First, you must calm the man who you call Father, or I will kill him too.

Another arrow sailed towards the bear. Father hadn't stopped trying to save me. So he did love me, after all. Despite everything, he had space in his heart for his abnormal child.

You are not abnormal. You are more precious than any of those simpletons. They do not appreciate you. They never have. But I do.

I turned from Eliki and waved my arms. "All is well, Father. The bear won't hurt me."

In response, Father nocked another arrow. "Mara, have you lost your mind?"

I will give you everything you desire, Mox, and so much more. All you must do is submit to me. Serve me and me alone.

"Serve you? How?" I asked.

Dedicate your life to me, and I will remake you into the image and form you so desire.

"How do you mean?"

To change one's form takes a great amount of skill. Many years will pass before you have the ability to change like me.

"How many years?"

As many as it takes.

I quivered at his reply. For a god, especially one who moved among worlds, time didn't mean the same as it did to us mortals. What if I spent my whole life striving for this changing art, never to succeed?

Do not worry, young one, when you are bound to the gods, you will find your life extends far beyond the years of mortal men, but you will never see your family or your village again.

"Mara!" My father scrambled down the boulders toward us.

Choose quickly, young Mox. This offer ends the moment your father reaches us.

Wasn't their offer what I always wanted? To leave home, to run away, and become like the god before me? But leaving behind my parents, my family and everyone I knew and loved? My heart ached, already aware of my response.

"Yes, I will."

The bear seemed to smile. *Yes, what?*

"I will be your servant and learn your ways. I will give up everything if you will teach me to be like you."

Then we are agreed.

A swirling wall of snow rose between my father and me before I could give him a proper goodbye. The god-bear took me between his paws and sunk his teeth into my shoulder. Agonizing pain roared through the left side of my body.

Do not scream, young Mox. You, too, must make your sacrifice. In order to travel between the mortal world and the world of the gods, I give you the body of this bear. When you aren't learning to become man or woman or both, you will be my eyes and ears in this bitter land. You will see things that mortal eyes cannot, and you will hear the call of children at night, children who feel lost and misunderstood.

I could not speak, could not protest as life bled from my mortal body. One moment, I gazed into the eyes of the god-bear, gasping for breath. The next, I saw the world from a new point of view. The thick fur covering my skin warmed me. My great muscles rippled beneath my snow-white hide. I could hear the beat of my father's racing heart, the scent of panic rising from his skin.

Now go, child. Venture far and wide so I can see those who creep through my brother's forests. There are others like you in the world. Together we shall find them, and I shall teach all to be more like me. Go north and instinct will guide you to the veil between this world and the next. And be wary of men. You are the most powerful beast in the forest, but you are not invincible.

A prick of pain roused me. The man who was once my father had sunk an arrow into the dense flesh above my shoulder. I found my feet, surprised at the speed with which I could move such an enormous body. I fled through the woods, charging through snowbanks tall as a man, until I could no longer pick up their stench.

At last, I allowed myself to slow. I thrashed my paw, still clumsy in my new skin, and tried to pry the arrow—Father's arrow—from my shoulder. The shaft splintered and blood seeped from the wound. The pain could not compete with the ache in my heart.

As the snow churned beneath my great paws, my lungs filled with a thousand scents, and I saw the world through transformed eyes. My new life would not be an easy one. I had known all along I would do anything to serve Eliki and couldn't wait to guide other lost souls toward my patron.

My life would be strange and hard, but I would prove myself to Eliki. And someday, even if far from that moment, I would finally become what I always wanted.

--T.J. Fier is a theatre professor, scenic artist, and set designer. You can find her work in the horror anthologies: *Nothing Short of Horror* and the 2022 edition of *Deathlehem*. Her first novel, *The Bright One*, will be re-released from Three Little Sisters Publishing in December of 2022. You can find her at **@iamfierless** on Twitter and Facebook. And at @tjfier_author on Instagram.

The First Law of Winter

By Marc de Celle

For me, snow existed in places people went to go skiing.

I'd never been through four seasons in my life. In Arizona, California, and Florida, where I'd lived until now, sure, it was hot in the summer. And it was cool in the winter, *sometimes* – the same way it's cool, sometimes, during the *summer* in Fargo, where we'd just moved. If you shut your eyes and tried real hard, in the places I'd spent my first fifty years, you could imagine there were two seasons – *Hotter* and *Cooler*. That worked pretty well until you opened your eyes, looked outside, and tried to figure out what time of year it was. Everything looked pretty much the same year-round. And we all lived inside air-conditioned spaces, from houses to offices to vehicles, a good nine months out of the year. So for me, the seasons had always been more an act of the imagination than of nature.

Snow had always been something to be visited. But now, it was about to be visited upon us.

In early October, people started asking, "Are you ready for winter yet?" At first, I thought this was a figurative sort of question, a sort of friendly Fargo shorthand for *Have you mentally braced yourself, warm-blooded novice?* But I soon realized it was much more. It was a deep and abiding concern for my family's survival.

This began to hit home sometime in early October, when a new acquaintance asked, "Do you have a snow blower?"

"A what?" I responded, brilliantly.

It quickly became clear that October was a time of fairly intense preparation for everyone around here, and I was woefully unprepared. Winter was coming, ready *or not*. There were an uncertain number of days before it hit, and a certain number of things had to be done before it did, or it would be *too late*. We could be in real trouble.

So October became busy. Buying winter clothes – hats, jackets, snow pants, socks and boots – for everyone, all good to at least twenty below. Bringing *everything* inside – barbeques, patio furniture, hoses, dog toys, *everything* – and getting it organized well enough to still walk through the garage, leaving room for our two vehicles. Getting a garage heater installed, so nothing out there would get completely frozen. Covering all the outside faucets so our plumbing wouldn't die a frozen death. Buying a snow blower, getting it put together and practice-running it, so my first time behind the handles wouldn't be in ten-below weather with the snow falling sideways in a twenty-mile-an-hour wind. Buying a generator and getting it primed and running, ready to go at a moment's notice in case of an extended power outage. Getting a custom dog house built around the outside of the doggie door so it wouldn't get covered over in the snow drifts to come. I even consulted the top Fargo engineer for Xcel, the gas company, and confirmed that if the power went out for a few days, as I'd learned it could when an ice storm topples major power lines, the natural gas would still flow. Then we went into town and picked out a nice gas fireplace, which was installed just in time, as it turned out.

Whew – we were ready. I hoped. October ended with our kids enjoying their first Fargo Halloween trick-or-treating with an occasional snowflake or two on their noses.

The first real test came in late November, a few days after our new fireplace had finally been installed. About mid-afternoon on Sunday the 28th, it started to rain, a cold rain that soon became a *freezing* rain – warmer upper clouds were releasing droplets, but a colder, lower layer had brought the temperature of everything on the ground – trees, streets, houses, everything – to below freezing. As soon as the rain hit, it turned to ice. And as we went to bed that night, it was still raining.

When we got up Monday morning, the rain had turned to sleet, which was blowing sideways in winds between twenty and thirty miles per hour – exact measurements were impossible, the television meteorologist reported, because all the anemometers were frozen over in ice. And all the schools were closed.

"Our first snow day! Yeah!" the kids chorused, then Austen added: "And it's not even snowing!"

That was about to change.

Midafternoon, the sleet turned to snow. The winds had picked up to about forty miles per hour, the meteorologist now guesstimated, with gusts even higher. We were in the midst of our first Fargo blizzard. For a while, we all stood at the big living room picture window. Nothing but white. Occasionally, a ghostlike image of the big trees across the street would appear briefly, then disappear in another gust of blowing snow. It was eerie, magical, and absolutely fascinating for the kids and me, whose eyes had never seen such things. My wife Charlene, who'd grown up loving Wisconsin winters, couldn't have been happier. By evening, she was fully settled in, warm and cozy by the fire, reading a book, cookies baking in the oven. She was home, and so were we all.

Little did I realize it was just the beginning. Only as the long, cold winter wore on would we discover how truly magical, warm and cozy a Fargo winter can be. The first revelation was right around the corner.

We slept in Tuesday morning. No one would be going anywhere for a while, local newscasters had assured us the night before. The snow and wind would settle down, but Fargo would be covered not just in a thick blanket of snow, but even more troublesome, beneath the snow would be layer upon layer of slick ice, first laid down by the freezing rain, then added to by the sleet that had followed. Even snowplows would have trouble navigating what promised to be *extremely* slippery streets. Fargo would be digging out for a while.

So it was about nine in the morning before I walked to the living room picture window and began pulling the cord to open the blinds. About halfway, I dropped the cord and simply stood in awe. The world outside, which had been green and gold just two days ago, then completely white yesterday, had once again transformed, this time into something completely unexpected – a silvery blue landscape with hundreds of sparks of golden sunlight glinting off of everything, sparks that shot and danced and glistened with even the slightest movement. The world was made of glass!

Breaking out of my reverie, I ran down and woke the kids. Soon we were out exploring this strange, new fairytale world. The sky was a cloudless azure, the sun a deep yellow. The snow, a foot or more deep, had a thin layer of microflakes on top iced just enough to scatter tiny points of sunlight in every direction. Even the stop sign at the corner of our street was beautiful, washed completely clean and covered in an inch-thick glaze of ice that made it look like a giant, delicious cherry-red lollipop sticking out of a whipped-cream world. Looking around, our whole neighborhood was strewn with glistening colored candy houses with generous helpings of white icing poured over them. Austen suddenly yelled, "We're walking on a giant *cake!*" and we all laughed. Best of all were the trees, covered in nearly an inch of clear-blue ice, shooting golden sparks of sunlight whenever they swayed ever so slightly, crackling – you could actually hear them – in the tiniest of breezes.

Wow. So the worst Fargo storms were actually – *the best!*

This was the first paradox of Fargo winter I discovered. But it was not the last. Nor the greatest. For I was soon to learn the law of winter in Fargo.

***

It was a February afternoon, a little over two months since our first magical winter storm. A light snow had been falling since morning.

I was a bit late getting home. *Charlene's probably been home about a half-hour already*, I thought, turning into our driveway.

As I walked into the kitchen, Charlene greeted me. "Hi, Honey! I got stuck in our driveway! I told you to snow blow the driveway before going out so it wouldn't build up *all day!*"

She had that half-quizzical, *Why didn't you listen?*, half-comical, *Because you were on Planet Marc!* look I know so well.

"If you got stuck, why aren't you still out there?" I asked.

Charlene whacked me on the shoulder, trying not to laugh. "Because a *neighbor* rescued me! He pushed the car back out onto the street, then drove his big snow blower over and cleared the driveway. Didn't you notice there isn't any snow on the driveway?

"Umm… Now that you mention it, I guess there should be snow on the driveway."

"You *think*?"

"On occasion," I said, "although this apparently isn't one of them." The kids started laughing. They'd moved into the kitchen as soon as they'd heard me come home. They loved the *dad's in trouble* routine, and I was grateful; Charlene can't resist breaking a smile when both our kids are laughing. She turned toward the counter to hide her face. I was supposed to be in *trouble*, not making everyone laugh.

My mind, however, was still on the story of Charlene's adventure. "So who rescued you?" I asked.

"I don't know his name." She turned around and pointed east, a little smile still showing. "He came from two houses down. He was out snowblowing his driveway when I got stuck. Next thing I knew he was over, smiling and pushing the car back out onto the street and telling me to wait. Then he ran back to his place and brought his big snow blower over and cleared out our entire driveway." She was looking at me, eyes wide, giving me her 'Can you believe *that*?' look. "I mean, what a *super* nice guy!"

That weekend, I made a point of introducing myself to our gallant neighbor two houses to the east, a North Dakota native named Chad. As I came to know him a little better over the next few years, I learned that Chad is one of those Northern Prairie, farm-raised guys who's remarkably capable and generous, but who never seems to notice how good – in every sense of the word – he is. When I brought him a thank you card our whole family had signed, he was all smiles, playing down his act of kindness, shaking his head, waving his hand dismissively, "Oh, it was nothing. *Really*."

And that's how Chad introduced us to the governing law of Fargo in winter:

The colder it is, the warmer it gets.

-- "The First Law of Winter" is excerpted and adapted from Marc de Celle's humorous regional bestseller *How Fargo of You*.

Spring Storm

By Barbara Bustamante

Spring has come with cool breezes

Curtains wave the coming warmth.

April fools a warning beseeches

Quite a shock to melting drifts.

The fog seen as silent mist

That lingers on through the night.

At morning light, the sun is missed

As gentle rain forms shallow pools.

Sheltered from the falling rain

Gave way to other plans and tasks.

Startling sounds from windowpane

Reveals show of sno-cone ice.

From sleet to flakes in no time at all

The world is covered in blanket white.

Breezes swirl as more flakes fall.

Where is vernal equinox?

As flakes gather and fill the sky

Big as biscuits floating by.

Breeze gave way to wind so spry

As snow in gusts blow side to side.

Darkness hides the light of day

Snow falls without end.

In sweet repose I must stay

To see the drifts in morning light.

I rise to hear a beeping sound.

By streetlights view a pickup truck

Moving snow across the ground.

Snow blowers casting streams of snow.

With sunrise creeping across the land

No snow, no wind, but silent cold.

Just thoughts of cooking eggs and ham

How best to spend a winter day?

-- Barbara Bustamante holds a BUS Degree in Food and Nutrition from North Dakota State University. She is semi-retired and lives in Moorhead, MN with her cat.

Snow By Any Other Name

By Tina Holland

Innocent, Minnesota

December 21st

Holly Frost was in trouble. She of all people should be able to make it snow. It was her job, though maybe it was more of a calling. Her current job was as a barista at Bear Tooth Tea & Coffee.

As a descendent of King Jack, she should be able to conjure snow in her sleep, but after a week of trying, she had failed. Now, the town would be in an uproar.

Her alarm continued to sound off as she stared out the window of her cabin in disbelief. Why wasn't this working? Had some witch or powerful fae put a curse on her?

Holly had four days to create the white fluffy stuff, or some variation thereof. Snow, sleet, flakes, powder, graupel, whatever name—she needed to get some on the ground. She would settle for heavy hoarfrost at this point.

Her first year making snow solo and she couldn't make it happen. Grandpa Jack thought she was ready, but maybe she needed help after all.

She wasn't about to let down the people, shifters, and fae of Innocent who depended on snow for their livelihood.

Holly turned off the blaring alarm and started the coffee pot. She would call her mom and see if the Frost family could send reinforcements.

She went to her closet and grabbed a pair of jeans, a t-shirt, and a sweatshirt that read 'You, Innocent U' for the local university. By the time she was dressed, there was enough coffee in the pot for a cup. She poured some and called her mother.

Her mother picked up on the second ring. "Holly, what's wrong?"

"Why should anything be wrong?" Holly couldn't help the defensiveness that crept into her voice.

"You only call when you need help." Her mother answered with a pragmatism Holly wished she had right now. Her nerves were frazzled.

"I do need help."

"What is it?"

"The snow. I can't make it snow."

"So Innocent is getting a little freezing rain. It's Yule. I'm sure you'll have snow by the end of the day." The confidence in her mother's voice was enough to make Holly think so, but she didn't dare risk it.

"There's no freezing rain." Holly sat in one of the white wicker chairs.

"Drizzle?"

"Nope." Holly sank deeper into the red cushion.

"A flurry?"

"Not even a frost," Holly confessed.

"Not even... Holly, what are you saying?" The pragmatism had been replaced with panic.

"My powers aren't working."

"Aren't working? Why aren't they working?"

"Mother, I wouldn't be calling you if I knew why?"

"Holly, you have to get snow on the ground."

"That's why I'm calling you. Can you send some help?"

"No, I can't. Your brothers and sisters have their own towns. Your cousins, aunts, uncles, and even your father and I have been assigned to multiple storm fronts. We gave you Innocent, Minnesota because… well…" Her mother stopped speaking. Eirwen Frost was rarely speechless.

"What?" Holly asked.

"Well, we gave you Innocent because Mother Nature usually blankets the state of Minnesota all on her own. It normally doesn't need a Frost monitoring it."

"You assigned me to a town that didn't need me?" Holly was too stunned to be hurt.

Her mother sighed. "Well, normally there is already snow on the ground."

"So, I'm a failure as a Frost." Holly experienced a sudden onset of nausea and sat down.

"You're not a failure. You just need a little help. There are plenty of powerful fae in Innocent to help you."

"There are?"

"Yes. Just check in with the local authorities and perhaps they can help you with this problem."

The local authorities? As in Sheriff Andy Finn. The bear shifter avoided her at all costs. Well, it wasn't her fault he didn't like the Frost family. She needed help, as did Innocent. So he would just have to suck it up and deal with her.

***

Sheriff Andy Finn watched as trouble—AKA Holly Frost—made her way towards him. What did the woman want? Why did she look as if she had him in her sights? All he wanted was to manage this town of shifters and humans and make sure everyone got along. Having the fae parked in his backyard didn't help, and he didn't want to tangle with them any more than necessary.

Andy had a job to do, and he did not need the distraction of Holly. It was bad enough he was still awake. As a bear shifter, he needed to hibernate, but his clock was off until the weather dropped below thirty-two degrees. It was nowhere near freezing, not even a frost—unless he counted the Frost standing in front of him.

"Sheriff," Holly sounded out of breath. "I need your help."

"How may I help her royalness?" He wasn't in the mood.

"Well, you could skip the attitude."

He cringed. It wasn't her fault he was attracted to her and went on the defense whenever she was near. "Sorry. I'm not sleeping well. "

"Now it's my turn to apologize. That is probably my fault."

She couldn't know thoughts of her kept him awake. He imagined kissing her and wondered what she might taste like, what running his hands through her auburn tresses and staring into her maple brown eyes would be like. He frowned as he tried to quell the image in his mind.

"I can see you're confused," she continued when he didn't speak. "I'm having problems making it snow."

"Is that why it's so warm?"

She nodded.

Warm was relative, but temps in the forties definitely qualified as warm in northern Minnesota this time of year.

"Did you call in another Frost?" He bristled at the thought of another one of her snobby cousins showing up. They had been assigned here before Holly took over last year. The last Frost, Bianca, was the reason he avoided Holly. Bianca thought she was better than the shifters and humans who resided in Innocent. Bianca had been so caustic that the town elders requested a replacement in January. Holly showed up during the spring thaw.

"I tried. They are managing a storm front away from here." She looked down at her feet, tapping her tennis-covered shoes together.

"Did you get the spell wrong?" he asked.

"There is no spell."

"How do you make it snow?" He was curious about Frost magic.

"It usually snows as I sleep."

"While you sleep?"

"Yeah. I think about the type of snow I want and when I dream it snows. "

"Have you created snow before?" It figured the town sent away the great Bianca and the Frosts replaced her with a novice.

"Yes! I'm not incompetent,"

"Do you feel okay?" He couldn't keep from being concerned.

"Yes, but..." She wouldn't meet his eyes and her posture slumped.

"What?"

She peered up at him. "I'm not dreaming."

"Of snow?"

"Of anything."

He slashed his hand through the air. "Holly, you aren't making any sense."

She sighed. "I'm sorry."

"What do you need me to do?" The sooner it snowed the sooner his deputy, a wolf shifter, could take over.

"I need to meet with the elders?"

"Are you kidding me? Most of them are gone for Yule."

"Okay, okay! I'll settle for Jaime Collins."

"She's in Atlantis with her husband."

"Are there any Elementals here?"

"Brigit Collins."

"Ugh! A fire elemental? No wind or water fae?"

"No. Chase Bridges transferred to Montana."

"Huh? I'm wondering if that might be why it hasn't snowed?"

He shook his head. "You just said it wasn't snowing because you weren't dreaming."

"That's true, but my mother said I was assigned here because it normally snows in Innocent without a Frost."

"Then why even assign one?" His patience was wearing thin.

She threw up her hands. "I don't know. All I know is that snow is not happening, and I need some help."

"Get in the squad car. We'll drive up to the Fireside Inn and talk to Brigit. Maybe she can help." He walked towards his car.

Andy heard Holly's sigh as she fell in step behind him.

***

After they were a few miles down the road, Holly debated for two seconds on confronting Andy about his issues. She decided if she had to live in this town for any length of time they would need to get along. "So, do you not like me because Bianca broke up with you?"

Tires squealed and slid as he stopped the car. "What!?"

Holly looked behind them. *Whew, no one on the road.* "You heard me. Is your animosity towards me because of Bianca?"

"How do you know about Bianca? Did she admit to dating a common bear?" he said.

She rolled her eyes. "Please, I work at Bear Tooth. There's more gossip there than at Mabel's Mane Salon."

"Do you know why the great Bianca broke up with me?"

Holly shook her head. She had no idea. Personally, she found Andy extremely attractive. Tall, dark, and handsome. Even if she didn't already know, his personality alone was enough to indicate he was a grumpy old bear. Maybe his grumpiness and her cousin's ice queen facade didn't match.

"At our breakup, Bianca informed me Frosts could only mix with a pureblood fae." His voice choked out.

"She said that?" Holly thought it was pretty rude of her cousin to trample on poor Sheriff Andy with her unfound prejudice.

"Yes. I'm surprised you don't share the sentiment."

"I'd have to put myself on the extinction list."

"What do you mean?"

"Jack Frost isn't even a pure fae."

"He's not?"

"No. He's one of a kind so it'd be impossible to find a mate like him. Actually, his first wife was human."

"First wife?"

"Yeah. Jack has had four altogether. Bianca's great grandmother was wife number two and a mermaid. Jack was married to her the longest. That branch believes they should keep the line pure and marry only wind and water fae. Not that it matters."

"So, your great-grandmother was a mermaid." He swirled his finger around. "La-di- frickin-da."

"My great-great-great grandmother was Jack's first wife. Bianca is older than me. She's like my grandparents' age."

He stared at her and looked as if he might speak. A honk behind them stopped him. Instead, he started the car moving again. They sat in silence for the remainder of the trip.

***

Holly learned that the Fireside Inn used to be named The Hotel. Apparently, Brigit Collins' late husband found it humorous to have the only establishment of its kind at the time named The Hotel. She shook her head at silly humans.

Except for the fireplace burning in the lobby, the inn was quiet as they entered.

"I'm in the kitchen," came a shout from the back.

Holly was happy Andy had brought her here. She hadn't had a chance to meet the elder woman yet, and she felt the warmth of holiday and hearth when they entered the kitchen. The smell of Krumkache reminded her of home.

"Hey, Mrs. Collins," Andy said.

"I've told you before Andy, you can call me Brigit."

"Sorry, ma'am, that doesn't feel right. Seems disrespectful." Andy seated himself on a barstool on the opposite side of the counter. Holly followed suit.

"Fine, fine." The woman continued pulling pastries off the hot iron and rolling them nimbly into cones with her hands. She nodded at

Holly. "And who is this?"

"This is Holly Frost. She's needing a bit of guidance from you."

Brigit finished her current pastry roll and wiped her hands with her apron. "You Jack's granddaughter?"

"Great-great-great granddaughter," Andy clarified.

Mrs. Collins stared hard at her. "The human line?"

Holly nodded.

"Good. I always liked that side of your family. We were happy that you were available to take on Innocent. Your grandfather Johann was here in the 1950s and was well-loved in the community.

"Thank you, ma'am. I'll let him know you appreciated his time here. He doesn't work much anymore," Holly said with all sincerity.

Bridget refilled a cup on the counter. "Coffee?"

"Yes, please," Andy answered.

"No, thank you, ma'am." Holly didn't want coffee. She wanted to figure out why she was broken.

Bridget passed a cup of coffee to Andy and leaned on the counter. "How can I help you?"

"She can't make it snow," Andy announced.

"Perhaps she'd like to tell me." Brigit shot him a dirty look.

"Sorry." Andy hung his head and sipped his coffee.

"He's right." Holly wasn't sure why she felt the need to defend Andy. "I've been having problems. My mother informed me that normally it snows here easily without a Frost."

Brigit seemed to be thinking. "Sometimes it does."

"Is that because you have a balance of Elementals?" Holly asked.

"Yes," Brigit answered.

"And now you're missing an Atlantean and wind elemental?"

"Actually, once you came on board, most of the elders took the holidays off, so you're actually missing some powerful fae, as well."

Holly turned to Andy. "Are there any fae on the city council?"

Andy shook his head. "The council is made up of humans and of those, I'm not aware of any who may practice the craft."

"I don't know how I'm going to make it snow. I don't understand. I've never had this problem before." Holly's head was heavy, so she settled it in her crossed arms on the counter. She wanted to cry.

"You're unbalanced," said Brigit.

Holly lifted her head. "I beg your pardon."

"You are out of balance. I can tell just by looking at you."

Andy swiveled his seat in Holly's direction. "You can?"

"Why wouldn't I be? I'm stressed beyond belief and I--"

"Have a crush," Brigit added before taking a sip of her cup.

Andy leaned in and whispered in Holly's ear. "On who?"

"None of your business." Holly sat up straight and pushed Andy away from her.

Andy looked at Brigit.

"I think she likes you." Brigit said matter-of-factly.

The fire elemental was going to be the death of Holly. She was going to expire from embarrassment. "I think we need to go." Rather than wait for Andy, she just got up and walked out of the inn.

***

"Go after her!" Brigit said.

"You can't be certain she likes me."

"I believe she does, although I can't understand why. You've been nothing but rude to her."

"I haven't."

"Andy, please. We've all seen how you've treated her. She's not Bianca."

"Does everyone know about Bianca?"

Brigit shrugged. "It's a small town."

He didn't know what to say. Brigit was right. He had not been polite to Holly since she arrived. He had Deputy Wolf handle any calls out to her cabin. Whenever she showed up at work, he left Bear Tooth rather than interact with her. And yet, on the car ride over Andy warmed to the knowledge that Holly wasn't a full-blooded fae. Could that mean she might be interested in a bear shifter?

"You're the reason it won't snow."

Andy swung his head up. "What?"

"You avoid her and push her off on others. How do you think that makes her feel?"

"Unbalanced?"

"Among other things."

"I know."

"Do you? You act like an ass whenever she's around. What would it hurt to be nice to her?"

"Nothing." Actually, given his newfound insights, it would be easier than Brigit thought.

"Then go after her."

"I will." He quickly followed Holly and ran into her just outside. He couldn't resist teasing her. "You like me?"

"It doesn't really matter does it?" She turned away from him and walked towards his car.

"What do you mean?" he asked.

"You're still hung up on Bianca? Aren't you?"

"No. Why would you think that?"

"Because she's taller, blond, blue-eyed, and beautiful. I mean I'm sure she broke your heart. My being here may remind you of her only because I'm a Frost..."

He needed to shut her up, so he did the only logical thing. He kissed her. She tasted like nutmeg and smelled like a fresh forest. He tugged her hips close to him.

Her hands wrapped around his neck.

A cool breeze caught the air and it smelled like snow.

He pulled away from her. "Did you do that?"

Her brown eyes blinked. "Do what?"

"The air. It just got colder." Yes, there was definitely a chill in the air.

As Holly stared up at him, a few snowflakes sprinkled her hair. The white reminded him of stars in a dark sky.

"It is colder." She stepped back. "I wonder why that happened."

"Maybe you are finding your balance?" he ventured.

"Maybe. You can take me home now."

"I have a better idea. Why don't you come to my cabin? I'll make you some dinner, we'll watch a movie and take your mind off trying to make it snow."

"Are you suggesting that it will just happen?"

"What can it hurt? We won't be any worse off than we are now."

"No. I really need to get home and figure this out."

***

They drove in silence back to her cabin. Holly wasn't sure what caused the scattering of snowflakes. Was it the kiss? She doubted it. Brigit Collins said she needed to find her balance. Andy's kiss had made her feel anything but. Her heart was racing, and her insides were melting like spring snow. There was no way the man would help balance her. Perhaps Mother Nature had finally taken pity on her and decided to help.

The Great Mother's assistance seemed far more likely than Holly having created the temperature drop and a few flakes after having failed so miserably in the past month.

When they stopped, Holly got out and had no idea where she was. "This isn't my cabin."

"I know. It's mine," Andy said.

"What are we doing here?"

"I asked you in the car if you minded stopping here for lunch before I take you back home. You said nothing, so I didn't think you cared one way or the other." He shrugged as if it was of no consequence.

"Sheriff, you've kidnapped me."

"Kidnapped you? I did nothing of the sort. I told you I have to feed Whiskers."

"Whiskers?" she asked.

"Yes. My cat!"

She giggled at the thought of such a large man owning a small animal like a cat.

"What?" He stared at her.

"You. I can't imagine you with a small creature such as a cat." It was more than she could resist, and the laughter came bubbling forth like a stream.

"I will have you know that Whiskers is a very masculine cat."

"I'm sure." She followed him into the house, trying to stifle her amusement.

"He is." His face soured at her.

Once she was inside, her eyes leisurely explored his cabin. Like hers, it had knotty pine, but where his cabin was one level she had a loft in her A-frame. She strolled through his kitchen, eyeing his porch and living room before freezing in her tracks. A sandy-colored cat with familiar whisps on its ears, black bars on its forelegs, and a bobbed tail stopped Holly in her tracks. The thing must be four feet long. "What is that?"

"That is my cat," Andy replied as if owning the beast was normal.

She stared at the creature now stalking her as if she was lunch. "That is not a house cat, it's a...a...What is it?"

Andy picked up the cat who seemed dwarfed in his large arms. Sometimes she forgot he was a bear shifter. "Whiskers is a bobcat."

"A bobcat? You domesticated a bobcat?"

"I didn't domesticate him. He's wild."

Holly took a cautionary step backward.

"You aren't afraid of him, are you?"

"No. No. Why don't I wait in the car?" She'd almost reached the door.

Whiskers chose that moment to leap between her and the door. He was definitely stalking her. The cat gave her an intent stare as if sizing up its next meal.

Holly stood straight and faced the animal. She took a gingerly step backward before bumping into Andy. "I'm sorry. I--" She froze when the animal grazed against her calf ready to...wind around her legs?

Whiskers wound figure eights around her legs, purring so loudly that the vibrations traveled across her limbs.

"I think he likes you," Andy said.

"Well, that's a relief," she said, dumbfounded.

"Let me feed him and then we can head back to your cabin."

Holly had almost forgotten she'd raised a bit of a snit earlier. "Oh, no, that's fine. Take your time."

He gave her a weird look. "Uh, okay. Have a seat."

Holly sat in a chair large enough for, well, a bear. She watched as said bear went to the cupboard.

Andy pulled out a can of salmon and opened it.

Once the sound of an opening can pierced the air, the cat no longer cared about Holly, for which she was immensely grateful.

She watched in fascination as Andy forked the salmon onto a plate and placed it at a bar in the kitchen. Whiskers jumped up on a barstool and proceeded to devour his food.

"Can I get you anything?" Andy asked.

Holly's stomach chose that moment to grumble. The cat lifted its head and looked at her. She'd swear it even smiled at her.

"I guess I'm hungry," she admitted.

"You are a vegetarian?"

"How'd you know?" Did bears read minds?

"Most fairies are."

"I suppose that's true, except the water fairies. Some of them eat fish."

"I have some vegan mac and cheese from when Bia…"

"When Bianca and you dated."

He nodded but said nothing as he turned away and prepared their meal.

There was something about watching a man cook that she found very sexy. Granted it was just mac and cheese, but she'd never had anyone consider her feelings, let alone her basic needs. The last human she dated thought that a trip to Tito's Tacos qualified as a date.

She stood. "This is not a date!"

Andy turned and stared at her. "What?"

Holly knew she was turning all shades of red. She hadn't meant to announce her opinion. Luckily, she didn't need to respond.

"Look, I'm just making you lunch, which is done by the way."

Sure enough, Andy held two bowls of what looked to be delicious, and one was for her. She couldn't very well turn him down. "Sorry." She plopped back down on the chair.

"Follow me." He walked out onto the porch where there was a table big enough to seat twelve. There were some chairs lined along the wall indicating that more could be seated if needed. On the other side of the porch were two lounge chairs similar to those in the main cabin, and a small table fit for a fairy with two chairs that looked like they were meant for a sidewalk café.

Andy sat at the tiny table. Holly followed his lead. They ate their food in silence. He stared cautiously at her the whole time.

"What?" she finally asked after nearly licking the bowl clean as Whiskers had done earlier.

"Are you sure you have enough fae in you to make it snow?"

"What do you mean?" Then she looked at the chairs, the metal twisting like leaves and vines, the heaviness of it. "These are wrought iron, aren't they?"

"Yes. Bianca couldn't sit in them."

***

In hindsight, perhaps he shouldn't have mentioned Bianca's name.

"You know, Sheriff, I'm sick and tired of you getting in my face about being a snotty fae Frost one minute and then not-frickin-fae enough the next. If I was unbalanced, which I'm not, you certainly aren't helping." She pointed her finger at him.

His throat was thick with guilt. She didn't deserve his half-assed attempts at help. "I'm sorry. I don't really understand much about fae or magic or any of that stuff."

"Clearly." She huffed and crossed her arms.

"What can I do to help?"

"Besides calling back all the fae from vacation and telling them I'm a complete failure?" She leaned back in the tiny chair and rested her chin on her chest.

"I'm not doing that because you aren't a failure."

"How can you say that? It's the first day of winter." She stood, threw her hands towards the window. "Does that look like winter to you?"

"No, but you have time."

"I do not! Did you not hear me? First day of winter!"

"Yeah, but humans are more forgiving. They want to finish their holiday shopping and are content to wait until the twenty-fifth or, better yet, the new year!"

"Oh, my goddess, if it doesn't snow by the New Year I will have to go into hibernation." She faced the window, but her head was down.

Andy wasn't sure what possessed him to rise from his chair, walk towards her and wrap his arms around her small frame, but it appeared to him as if she could use a bit of his strength.

Holly leaned back against him. "I don't know how to fix this, Andy."

She'd used his given name rather than her 'Sheriff.' He kissed the top of her head and whispered. "Don't fix it."

She turned in his arms. "Don't fix it? How can you say that? You of all people can't go into a hibernation cycle until the temperature dips below freezing."

"How do you know that?"

"I grew up with bear shifters in Alaska."

"You did?"

"Yeah, my cousins."

He gripped her about the shoulders. "Did you say cousins?"

"Yes. My mother is a bear shifter, although she's polar and they don't really hiber-" She ended on a squeak as he lifted her up and carried her to the living room sofa before setting her down next to him.

"Andy." There was his name again on her lips. "What are you doing?"

"You're a bear shifter."

"No. I'm a Frost. We don't shift. The Frost blood is stronger than…"

"Shifter?"

"Yes, Frost blood is stronger than shifter." She smiled at him.

He couldn't resist. He gathered her into his arms snuggly and dipped his head to capture her lips.

***

Oh, Goddess! Andy was kissing her again. Her balance shattered with his hunger. He moved his mouth over hers in a slow devouring kiss. His arrogance that she 'Do nothing' was maddening. And yet she found this soothing. How many times had she dreamed of being crushed in his embrace? How devastated she was when she'd found out Bianca had gotten to him first.

Andy broke off the kiss. "Holly, what's wrong?"

She barely managed to answer. "Nothing."

"Do you always purse your lips into a thin line and frown when you kiss, or is it just me?"

"No, no, no! It's not you. It's Bianca."

"Excuse me?" He pulled away from her.

"I was just thinking how she got to you first."

"Are you jealous?" He winked at her.

"No. It's just that she seems to ruin everything she touches, except for, of course, snow."

He stood. "So, I'm ruined. Damaged goods."

"No. Don't get your fur all ruffed. I don't mean it in the way that you think. If anything, she ruined me for you." She gestured between them.

"I don't follow."

"Admit it. You didn't like me simply because I was a Frost."

He hung his head low. "I thought you would be like her."

"That's what I mean. I mean I guess I'm sort of thankful you aren't still hung up on her."

Suddenly he was kissing her again, crushing his lips against hers. Silencing her.

She pushed against him. "Stop that!"

He leaned back, giving her a devastating smile. "I don't know. It seems to be an effective method to keep you from spouting drivel."

Holly agreed her cousin was drivel, so she changed the subject to their current problem. "What about the snow?"

He looked out the window. "It seems to be managing itself out."

Sure enough, there were a few sprinkles floating outside. Holly walked to the window for a closer look. It wasn't really snowing. The flakes were translucent, but they were coming down enough that perhaps it could qualify.

Andy came to stand beside her. "Perhaps you'd been overthinking it."

"And stressing myself out," she agreed.

"Do you have to get back to your cabin?"

"Why?"

"I thought perhaps we could have popcorn and watch movies."

"W-O-O-F plays those holiday movies this time of year." Would he watch those small-town holiday movies with her?

He shrugged. "Okay."

Andy walked a few steps to the kitchen to make popcorn.

Holly grabbed the remote off the coffee table, turned on the TV and punched in 16.1 for the local station, W-O-O-F. "One is already playing. Oh, this one is cute—Santa's Snowbirds."

Andy peeked from the kitchen. "Is that the one where the old couple leaves the small town every Christmas and the residents start to believe they are Mr. & Mrs. Claus?"

"You've seen it?" A man who watched corny Christmas movies?

"A few times. My mom likes those movies too. Hey, do you want hot chocolate?" he hollered over the popping corn.

"Yes, please." He might as well ask if she wanted a mani-pedi with massage.

Once Holly settled in with her cup of hot chocolate and a bowl of popcorn between them, the air took on a chill and she shivered.

"You can lean in if you want?" Andy lifted his arm and nodded to his side.

She paused. It was tempting but--

"Or there's an afghan my mom made on the chair over there."

Holly set down the popcorn and hot chocolate then picked up the throw. "I'll curl up next to you too, if that's okay."

He smiled wide. "That is more than fine."

And Holly spent the afternoon watching movies and sipping hot chocolate while curled in Andy's arms.

Their fingers touched when they both reached for popcorn.

Andy made a game out of kissing her when the hero and heroine would kiss on the screen. He missed one and she was going to say so, but she looked up and found him sleeping. Rather than wake him, she snuggled closer and listened to his rhythmic deep breathing before she too succumbed to sleep.

***

Andy woke with a stiff neck. He went to stretch but found his arm wouldn't move. It was wedged between the couch and Holly. He lifted it to curl the appendage about her shoulder.

She stirred and, after a bit of struggling, finally opened her eyes. "Andy?"

"I'm here."

"What time is it?" Holly rubbed her eyes.

He glanced at his watch. "Just after eight."

She stood straight up. "Oh no. I better go."

"I don't think that's possible." He reached for her but succeeded only in grabbing handfuls of air.

"What do you mean?" She frowned.

"Look outside, Frost."

She rushed to the window. "There must be two and a half feet out there."

He walked to her side. "That would be my guess."

"Oh no! I went from no snow to...to...trapping people in their homes."

"No one is trapped." He wanted to reassure her. "The locals love snow. Now the bears can hibernate. The wolves can start up their dog sled business. The rinks can open. You did a good thing, Holly." The temptation was too much to resist so he gave up and hugged her.

She gave him a weak smile. "I guess you can finally hibernate."

"I can, but I found I don't need snow to hibernate."

"You don't?"

"No. I just needed a little Frost." Andy said before dipping his head and capturing Holly's lips.

She teetered. "You aren't helping my balance."

He swooped her into his arms. "Don't worry. I'll catch you."

"Maybe that's all I need," she replied.

-- Tina studied journalism at University, then went to work for a fortune 500 company working Logistics for over 20 years. She now writes full-time and helps her husband run his crop-dusting business in the summer. When she's not writing she likes to travel, read, and spend time with her family and friends. You can learn more about Tina at www.tinaholland.com.

Roadside Assistance
By Donna R. Wood

"Are you kids sure you don't want to stay the night, and head back in the morning?" Peggy asked, as she pulled her wool coat just a little tighter around her waist.

"Thanks, Mom, but Andrew's parents are expecting us for the gift-opening first thing in the morning. We'll be fine. It's only forty miles, and the storm's supposed to stay to the south." Megan flashed a half-smile, and squeezed her mom as though it might be the last time she ever saw her. "Merry Christmas, Mom. Love you," she whispered. "And tell Daddy I love him too."

Megan hated winter storms. Oh sure, the snuggly fireplace and hot cocoa scenes in the movies are great, but in Minnesota it's different. A lot different. The snow is the least of anyone's worries, really. It's the wind that causes most of the trouble. An open stretch of highway can ice over in a very short time, and then there's the black ice, and the cold…the bitter, bitter cold carried by the wind.

"Thank you for dinner, Mrs. Krage. It was very nice to meet you, and I look forward to seeing you on New Year's Eve," Andrew said, as he and Megan made their way down the driveway to the car.

Andrew pulled the door open for Megan, and waited for her to get in, before slamming the door. It was the one thing where Megan found herself conflicted about Andrew. None of her friends' boyfriends held doors for them, or pulled out their chairs at the table, or showed any kind of chivalry in the least. It was nice, and embarrassing, at the same time. Although deep down, she loved it. Andrew had been her knight in shining armor since the first time they had met. She smiled to herself as she remembered Andrew punching Ryan, laying him out on the floor under the tables. Ryan had learned to keep his hands to himself, and never made any moves on Megan again. Yes, Andrew was her chivalrous, valiant knight, and she loved him for it.

The click of Andrew's seatbelt brought Megan back to the present. "Well, I told you that she would love me," Andrew beamed as he shifted into Drive. "And I think it's the beginning of a beautiful friendship between me and your dad. Who knew we would have so much in common?"

"Yeah, I guess maybe I really did find someone just like dear old Dad," Megan laughed. "Just wait until he gets you out on the big lake in the middle of January. You probably shouldn't have told him how much you like ice fishing. He's very serious about it, and he hasn't had anyone to go with since Lenny died."

"But I do like ice fishing, and hockey, and snowmobiling," Andrew said, taking a quick glance at Megan.

The sun had set nearly an hour before they had left the Krage's, and the dark of the depths of winter seemed to creep across the fields. The usual blanket of stars in the night sky had been replaced by an ever-darkening grayness that faded to black in the distance. The giant snowflakes that had begun to flutter down like a snow globe had turned into tiny flashes of light that whizzed in front of the windshield like a scene from Star Wars. The haunting howl of the increasing winds seeped into Megan's skin, and she suddenly felt scared. Maybe they should have stayed the night after all. It was now apparent that the storm had shifted and was about to bear down full force on them.

"Andrew, maybe we should go back. I'm kinda scared," she said, as she gripped the seatbelt that lay across her chest with one hand and the door handle with the other.

Not taking his eyes off the road, Andrew replied, "Don't worry. We'll make it. Besides, we're halfway there already. Let's just listen to some music and try to relax." Andrew fumbled with the knob, finally turning on the radio, which was ironically playing *I'll Be Home for Christmas*.

Both laughed, and then joined in the chorus. Maybe it was out of familiarity, or perhaps a sort of reassurance to themselves that they would be home for Christmas, despite the storm. The sing-along continued until the silhouette of a small animal appeared in the headlights. Andrew panicked. He slammed the brakes, and swerved to miss whatever it might have been, sending the car into a perpetual spin, careening down the highway, until it came to a stop in snow up to the floorboards.

Andrew clutched the wheel with both hands, as his heart came to a rest in his throat, and his lungs gasped for air. One by one, he peeled each of his fingers from their death grip on the steering wheel, then patted both of his arms. He didn't seem to have any injuries. His attention turned to

Megan in the seat next to him, who seemed to be staring blindly out the windshield in front her.

With a gloved finger, Andrew poked Megan in the shoulder. "Megan, are you okay?"

A brief silence hung in the air before she managed a weak, "Yeah. Yeah, I'm okay. I think." She ran her gloved hands over her face, down both arms, and across her lap. "Yes. Are you?"

"Yeah. I'm good. You stay here, and I'll go for help," Andrew said, while he started to open the door.

Megan grabbed him by the arm, pulling him back into his seat. "Get back in here. What's the matter with you?" she shouted. "You know the first rule of winter survival is to stay with your vehicle."

"We can't just sit here and hope someone comes along. It's freezing out there!" Andrew started to push the door open again, only to discover the snow outside was so deep the door wouldn't open.

"Exactly! It's freezing out there. And, besides, there's no one around for miles. Everyone's either at home with their families or at candlelight services. We just have to try to stay alive until the storm passes, and a state trooper comes with help. How much gas do we have?" Megan surprised herself with her take charge attitude. She always felt like she would be the one to panic in an emergency, and here she was bold and confident.

Andrew glanced at the gas gauge. "We have almost a full tank. I filled up when your dad and I went to get the milk."

"Okay. That's good. At least we won't freeze to death, if we play our cards right," Megan said, fishing her cellphone out of her purse. She gave it a disgusted look and put it back. "No service," she said. "The storm must have knocked out the cell towers."

It started as just a small chuckle and grew into a full-on laughing fit. Andrew couldn't help himself. He didn't know what else to do. Here they were out in the middle of nowhere, stuck in a snow-filled ditch, alone on Christmas Eve. It was like one of those cheesy holiday movies come to life.

Andrew's contagious laughter infected Megan, who began to giggle and even snort a time or two. As the gravity of their situation set in, the silence grew between them. In the movies, there was always someone who came along to save the day. They both knew that this could have a much different ending.

Megan snuggled against Andrew's arm, "Andrew, what are we gonna do?"

"Well, first, I'm going to get out and clear the snow away from the exhaust pipe, so we can run the car," he said, as he gave the door a hard shove with his shoulder.

Taking the scarf from around her neck, Megan held it out to him. "Here take this. Wrap it around your face."

He gave silent thanks that no one would see him with his head wrapped in Megan's red Christmas scarf, with its flecks of silver thread, and tassels that hung from the ends. Andrew trudged through the knee-deep snow to the back of the car. He wasn't sure if the car was on or off the road. He only knew that it was stuck, and stuck good. No amount of shoveling would get them out, even if he did have a shovel. Which he didn't because he never thought this would happen to him. After all, he was a good driver with no tickets and no accidents.

Andrew dug like a dog around the rear of the car until he had cleared all the snow that had surrounded it. He made sure there was no snow plugging the exhaust pipe, then hurried back to the warmth and safety of the car's interior. He peeled the scarf that was layered in ice and snow from his face and rubbed his cheeks with his bare hands to warm them.

"Where's your winter survival kit?" Megan asked, while she watched Andrew shiver in his now wet jacket and pants.

Through chattering teeth, he replied, "Um, there's a blanket in the trunk and some other stuff. There might be a couple of stale chocolate bars or something if you're hungry."

Megan slid over the console between the bucket seats into the back, pulled down the backseat, revealing the contents of the trunk. She pulled the blanket and the roll of garbage bags through the opening. "Take off your clothes," she said.

"I realize we might die, but are you serious? You want to do it now? What if help comes?" Andrew said, shocked by her words.

"No, you idiot. I want you take off your wet clothes, so you can get warm" she replied, a little annoyed with Andrew's lack of survival skills. The knight's shining armor was starting to show its tarnished places.

Andrew struggled to get the bulky winter jacket off, pulling his arms this way and that, until finally he was free. He threw it on the front seat and then slipped his shirt off over his head. Megan handed him a garbage bag that she had ripped a hole in the bottom for his head and one on each side for his arms. "Here, put this on."

"Mmmm…lemony fresh." He smiled, poking his head through the hole.

"Now take off your pants."

"Yes, ma'am." He slipped his snow covered pants off and threw them on top of his winter jacket. "Now what?"

"Your socks," Megan replied.

It wasn't until then that Andrew realized his socks were drenched from the snow and ice that had soaked through his shoes. He pulled them off, casting them onto the growing pile of wet clothes.

Clad only in the garbage bag and his boxers, Andrew sat facing backward in the front seat. "And now?" he asked.

"Now, get back here and we'll keep each other warm under this blanket," Megan said.

Side by side, snuggled under the blanket, they sat listening to the wind howl outside. It was an eerie, almost foreboding sound. Unnerving to say the least.

Megan wiggled out from under the blanket. "I'm going to turn the radio on," she said as she reached over the console between the front seats.

It was nearing midnight, and they hadn't seen a single vehicle on the road the entire time. Megan knew that her mom would be worried by now. Megan was supposed to text her when they got home, which should have been hours ago. This was the one time she hoped her mom was worried; worried enough to call the police and have someone out looking for them.

"Megan…" Andrew started.

"Yeah."

"You do know that when I say I love you, I really mean it, right?"

"Yeah, I know. I love you too. More than…" Megan's voice trailed off into her own thoughts. What if they didn't get home? What if they weren't home for Christmas? Would someone come looking for them in time? What if they were found frozen under the blanket in the backseat? How would her mom ever get through it?

Andrew drew Megan closer as a shiver rushed through his body. It seemed as if it were getting colder inside of the car, despite the running heater. "Tell me about your favorite Christmas," he said.

"Well, it's definitely not this one." Megan laughed a little. "I guess it was the one when I was seven and our whole family was together. Grandma, Grandpa, all my aunts and uncles and their kids. We all went ice skating on the lake." Megan chattered on about the holidays from days long past. She talked about all the food, the fights, and the love that seemed to permeate throughout the years.

Andrew's head began to bob up and down, as he fought to keep his eyes open. "I am so tired," he mumbled.

"No!" Megan shouted at the top of her lungs. "You can't go to sleep. Please, please don't go to sleep," she whimpered.

"I'm just gonna take a little nap. I won't sleep for long. I promise. I just can't keep my eyes open anymore."

"No! If you go to sleep, you won't wake up at all. Please stay awake with me. Please," she pleaded, while she scrambled to the front seat and turned the radio up louder. "Let's just sing Christmas carols."

Andrew did his best to keep up with the words floating out of the speakers, but with every song it became more and more difficult to stay awake. He started to feel warm again, as though the storm were no longer raging outside.

Tears rolled down Megan's face as Andrew drifted off to some unknown place. "God, please don't let him die. Please. I'm sorry for everything that I have ever done that made you mad, but please don't take him. I need him. I really, really do. Please don't take him." She nestled close to Andrew's side, and sobbed into his chest, while she listened to his heartbeat. This was it. This was going to be how it all ended. Not just for Andrew, but for them both. It was beyond hope now. All hope was lost. No one was coming for them. No one was going to save them. She let her own eyelids lower as she drifted off into an unknown place of her own.

***

The lids of Megan's eyes popped open as she felt the car moving backward. She shook Andrew to wake him. "Wake up! Wake up! We're moving!"

Andrew struggled to wake up. It was still dark. The wind was still howling. The snow was still falling, but they were moving. He looked down at himself, and realized he was still only wearing the garbage bag and his boxers. He snatched his clothes and shoes from the front seat, scrambling to put them on. There was no way, Christmas or not, he was going to be found by anyone in just his underwear! No amount of goodwill in the world would ever let him live that down.

Together, they peered out the rear window to see who was rescuing them. Andrew withdrew and reached for his winter jacket. "I don't see any lights. Get down and hide under the blanket," he whispered as he slipped his arms into the sleeves of his jacket. He crawled into the front seat and slunk down as far as he could, hoping not to be seen. Once they were back on the road, maybe he would be able to drive away.

He could hear the weirdest clicking noise outside of the window but couldn't quite make out what it was. Maybe it was just ice hitting the window. Maybe it was something to do with the way the car was being pulled out of the ditch. It sure was weird though. Clickity click. Clickity click. Over and over.

He noticed that the engine wasn't running, which was odd, because there was still over three-quarters of a tank of gas. Maybe the battery had died. Unlikely, but it could have happened, he supposed. The sound of the snow scraping the undercarriage grated on his nerves. It was a horrible noise accented by the clickity clicking. He tried to peer out the driver's side window, but every time it would fog over from the warmth of his breath.

"Do you see anything?" Megan's muffled voice came from under the blanket.

"No. Nothing. Shhhh. I can't see anything or anyone," he whispered.

They couldn't have been that far off the road. It seemed like an eternity before they came to a stop. Silence filled the car as they waited. Just what they were waiting for, neither of them knew. Andrew held his breath as he bobbed up and down to peek over the steering wheel. He heard a rapping noise on the window beside him. He closed his eyes, sucked in his breath, and turned his head to see who was out there.

Large black eyes that filled most of an odd-shaped head seemed to bore down into the very depths of Andrew's soul. It was hideous and fascinating all at the same time. It was like a train wreck, horrible but he just couldn't look away. All the air in Andrew's lungs seemed to be sucked out all at once. He couldn't move or speak or think.

The creature standing outside the car raised its three fingered hand and motioned for Andrew to roll down the window. Andrew's fingers searched for the window button, but nothing happened. The engine was off. He heard a voice, mostly in his head, that said, "Hey, buddy, pop the hood."

It was a dream. That was it! He had fallen asleep, and it was nothing more than a dream. There was no creature outside the window. They were still stuck in the ditch, and he was most likely freezing to death while he slept. Except he couldn't wake up. He heard the voice again, "Hey, buddy, pop the hood."

Unable to wake from the dream, Andrew reached for the hood release and pulled. He felt the familiar jerk of the car as the hood came loose. He watched as it rose in front of the windshield and he saw what he swore were the silhouettes of two human-like creatures, leaning over the side of the car, examining the engine compartment. He heard the clanking of metal on metal, interrupted by only the clickity clicking from before.

Megan stuck her head between the front seats to get a good look at what was happening. "Who are they?" she asked.

"I'm not sure, but my guess is aliens. I mean this is a dream and those appear to be aliens fixing the car," Andrew replied matter-of-factly, certain that he was, indeed, dreaming.

Slipping her hand out from under the blanket, Megan pinched Andrew's face, "Ouch!" he yelped.

"It's not a dream, Andrew. There really are aliens out there fixing the car. Who knows what they're going to do to us when they're finished?"

Another rap on the driver's side window, and Andrew heard the familiar voice. This time saying, "Give it a try. Turn it over."

Andrew obeyed the voice, turned the key in the ignition, and the engine came to life. Turning to Megan, who had climbed into the front seat, he said, "Hang on!" as he shifted the car into Drive and pushed the gas pedal to the floor. The engine revved, but the car stayed right where it was.

Again, the rapping came on the window. The creature outside motioned for Andrew to roll down the window. Andrew reached for the window's control button and rolled it down.

Both Megan and Andrew could hear the creature's voice in their heads as it spoke to them. "Looks like you hit the ditch hard. What are you doing out here on a night like this? Lucky, we came along when we did."

"Yeah, just lucky, I guess," Andrew replied. He couldn't believe that he was having a real live conversation with an alien. Encounters like this never ended well for the humans. Not in any of the documentaries he'd ever seen anyway. Yet, here they were, having a normal, everyday conversation.

The creature leaned on the car with his elbow resting comfortably on the window ledge. "You know, we almost didn't come this way tonight, on account of the storm and all, but here we are, and here you are."

Megan tried hard to wrap her head around what was happening. "Why did you help us? I mean, don't you usually abduct humans and run unspeakable experiments on us and stuff like that?"

"Well…now…it is Christmas after all, and it just didn't seem right to spoil it for you, just because we can," the creature replied.

An awkward silence filled the air between the creature and the humans in the car.

"Thank you for your help. If it hadn't been for you, we probably would have frozen to death out here," Megan said.

The creature clickity clicked to the others, signaling they should go back to wherever they had come from. "It's been nice chatting with you, but we have things to do tonight. You know, humans to abduct, experiments to conduct, and stuff like that. We're running behind schedule now, so we have to go."

"It was nice to meet you, and thanks again," Andrew said.

The creature turned and started to walk away, then suddenly turned back. "By the way, Merry Christmas, and you can tell them whatever you want, but they're never going to believe you!" The creature seemed to disappear into thin air, leaving both Megan and Andrew disbelieving themselves.

-- Donna R. Wood began her career as an author in 2011, when she published her first full-length novel, *Sticks and Bones*. Since then, she has gone on to write three novels and several short stories. Donna is a certified wellbeing coach and is the owner of Butterfly Phoenix and Butterfly Phoenix Publishing. Donna is a supporter of women's rights, an LGBTQIA2S+ ally, an interfaith minister, and coffee connoisseur. She makes her home in Fargo, North Dakota, where she enjoys spending time with her children and grandchildren.

Hoar Frost
By Brandi Malarkey

When I was young, I thought that "hoar frost" was "whore frost" and I couldn't understand what the silent and shimmering outdoor splendor had in common with the women my mother nudged me away from in the drugstore. The women who laughed loudly with each other as they bought red nail polish and tested lipstick on their hands. The women I secretly thought were the most beautiful I had ever seen.

Over time I learned that "whore" meant any woman who acted differently than the one my mother was trying to turn me into as she tried to clip and sculpt me into a shape I couldn't see with my own eyes. The nebulous "lady" who does not wear feathered hats that flow as she moves, or costumes that sparkle like ice in the light. Who learns to be less and less as she grows older.

Is it so very wrong to coat the surface occasionally? To wear a garment of frozen water and sunshine, or to unapologetically reach to the sky and say, "Here I am!"? For the world to catch its breath, seeing the ordinary become extraordinary for a small miracle of time? Is it so very wrong to be lit up with wonder?

I am no longer young, and I have learned that "whore" is used to dismiss many who dare to sparkle and flash and glimmer. Who do not seek their reflection in other people's eyes. Who adorn themselves with dreams or hope or bright red lipstick.

Perhaps "whore frost" was not so very wrong, after all.

Nature is unstifled and unashamed.

-- Brandi Malarkey is a multi-disciplinary artist, writer, administrator, and occasional hot mess. She is a collector of dead bugs and good books, and a believer that ordinary miracles and small kindnesses have the power to change the world. Learn more about Brandi on her website: www.itsallmalarkey.com

Frozen in Time

By Lyn Stoltenow

Uff da! Oh, for funny!

Ole and Lena walk into a bar.

North Shore. North Star.

The land of the free and the home of the brave.

Hot dish. Potlucks.

Is that near the Cities? Let's go to the mall.

Is it cold enough for ya? Ya know what they say —

Cold keeps the riff raff out.

Cold, hard as pavement, biting my cheeks

So cold I can't breathe

So cold I could die in the mean streets of Minnesota Nice

Frozen in time

In the Great White North

-- Lyn Stoltenow lives in rural Minnesota.

Frost

By Susette Quinn

The *tick, tick, tick* of the electric baseboard heat welcomes me awake. Behind the blinds, the sun is rising. I stagger into the kitchen to click on the coffee pot, an ancient Mr. Coffee I inherited when my mom passed.

It snowed yesterday and the world outside the window is a dazzling, pearlescent white. Deciding to skip my shower until after I get my shoveling workout, I put my hair in a braid to keep it out of my face and under my hat then I wander into the kitchen. The coffee maker has already gurgled a few cups into the carafe. I grab the creamer from inside the refrigerator door. Add creamer followed by the coffee. No stirring needed this way. I put the creamer in the door where it came from and carry my mug to the bedroom.

Last night's weather report mentioned a cold snap that would directly follow the new snowfall. Having grown up in the Midwest, I know this blindingly, brilliant sunshine means it is not fit for man nor beast out there. I grab my phone for the forecast and discover that it is -18 degrees Fahrenheit with a wind chill of over -30.

While sipping coffee, I dig out a pair of leggings because I am too stubborn to buy long underwear, a pair of sweatpants, a t-shirt, a hooded sweatshirt, and a pair of fleece socks. This day calls for layers.

In the mudroom closet that doubles as my laundry room, I find the boots my daughter gave me for Christmas a few years ago, a winter jacket with a company logo on it from a previous employer, scarf, stocking cap and double-layered fleece mittens. Once bundled with only my eyes visible, I fix my sights on the side door of the garage where the shovel that I put out months ago in preparation for days like these is resting. I shuffle through the ankle deep, fluffy powder to the door. I grab the shovel and start working my way out, pushing the snow away from the building.

The scraping of the shovel across pavement is deafening in the early morning crispness. I stop when I hear another sound. Out of the ordinary. I wait. Nothing. I continue removing the six or so inches from the sidewalk. There it is again. A whimper? Sniffle? I hold still so as not to rustle my layers. Quiet. Hmm, maybe I am hearing something, or maybe this is it and I am finally losing my mind.

I start removing the fluffy white stuff from the cement, throwing it as far as I can. Days this cold are not my favorite. Frost forms on your scarf and eyelashes, and your nose will freeze shut if you inhale too hard. Exposed skin burns, and your fingers will inevitably go numb. The upside is the gorgeous rainbow halo around the sun called a sun dog. If you need a silver lining, that, compared to the brilliance of the sun's reflection, would be it.

As I move along the length of the garage door, there's a disturbance in the snow. I can't tell what made the impressions, just that it happened while snowing. I peer closer to investigate and hear the whimper again. Definitely not losing my marbles. The garage door's weather stripping is loose, and it cannot be a coincidence that something has upset the snow there. I lean the shovel against the metal siding and follow my newly cleared path to the side of the garage.

The garage is warmer than the outside, but not much. Shimmying around the car to the second stall, I am surrounded by the hodgepodge of my lawnmower, patio furniture, flowerpots, and everything else I drag inside either at night or for inclement weather.

I stand still for a moment. There! A tiny cry. Sounds like it may be burrowed between the patio furniture cushions. I don't want to scare whatever is in here, or myself, so I move slowly.

Peering out from under a pillow is the face of a tiny, grey kitten, wet and frozen with frost on its whiskers. I don't want to spook it, but I need to get it inside and see if it was able to find shelter before frostbite set in.

I cautiously traverse the five or so feet between me and the chaise. The kitten cries out again but doesn't make a move. I coo and baby talk to it as I approach. The kitten tries to shrink back underneath the pillows but doesn't seem to have the strength to run or dart.

"Hey there, tiger. It's pretty chilly out here," I murmur as I crouch. "We need to get you warmed up. Will you trust me?"

The kitten lets me run a finger over its head while I whisper sweet nothings. I slide a hand under the kitty's ribcage and gently lift it out from under the pillows. There is no collar or tag. A quick look tells me the edge of its ear may be frostbit. I will check the pads of its feet when we are inside. I gently tuck it inside my jacket for the walk to the house.

Once inside, I grab a few towels out of the laundry hamper, toss them into the dryer and kick on the heat. I tug my mittens out of my pockets, unwrap my scarf, flop all my winter gear except the coat on top of the dryer, and work on kicking off my boots. I tuck a hand inside my jacket to hold onto the tiny bundle while shaking off my jacket and add it to the growing pile on top of the dryer.

I open the dryer and pull out the towels. Warm, not hot. Exactly as I had hoped. I swaddle the cat and we pad into the living room. I use one towel to keep it covered and another to carefully blot away any wetness caused by the thawing. This poor baby lets out a meow of thanks and snuggles deeper into the warmth. The ear, shriveled and curled on the tip and looking pretty raw, shows some definite damage. I am careful not to touch it. I will need to call a vet very soon. I glance at each leg and foot as this poor creature relaxes and falls asleep in my arms. The pads look okay but I am no expert. I am curious as to whether it is a boy or a girl. I sneak a peek. A girl.

"I wonder who you belong to and how you ended up with me?"

Mrs. O'Leary, a grandmotherly woman whose home faces mine, knows everything. She will know who is missing a cat. I pick up my phone and search for her number. She answers on the second ring.

"Mrs. O'Leary, this is Dana, from across the street. How are you this bright and snowy morning?"

"I am fine. I'm fortunate enough to have raised a houseful of boys so someone will be by to take care of moving my snow. I picked up groceries a few days ago when I heard about the drop in temperature. I sense you have something else on your mind though, Dana. What's going on?

"Ha! You always know and you're always right. I found a stray cat hunkered down in my garage when I was out shoveling. You don't know if anyone's pet has gotten out, do you? She's pretty small, grey and from the looks of it, exhausted."

"I haven't heard a thing, but I will ask around for you. A trip to the vet will tell you if she has a microchip or not. If I am bold enough to say -- and I am -- I have a feeling you have a cat now."

"I've never been a cat person, but I do love animals. I'm going to have to figure out food and a litter box until I can get to the vet."

"The boys will be here in an hour or so. They used to have a cat. Let me see if they have anything they aren't using any longer. I'll be in touch."

"That's very kind of you. Thanks. I'll talk to you later."

It is still too early to call a vet and I have the rest of the shoveling to do, but in all honesty, I could spend all day snuggling this little girl. Who knew I would like a cat? She is sleeping so soundly, I arrange her, all warmly bundled, on my favorite chair while I bring out a shallow bowl of water. Frost hasn't moved. Damn! I named her. They always say if you name them, they are yours. Hopefully this little girl has a microchip and a distraught owner.

Staring at her isn't doing me any good so I decide to finish the shoveling. If I am lucky she will sleep till I return. I place my bundled Frost on top of a folded blanket, and I tiptoe out the door to shovel.

My wet clothing is freezing fast, and with renewed motivation, I move with a speed I didn't know I had. Finishing the length of the driveway, I swear to myself that I will buy a snowblower or hire someone, then I start on the sidewalk.

As I begin the home stretch to the front door for the postal service, a truck comes down the street. The sounds are amplified in the cold temperatures, and I hear it long before I see the black king cab Ford. It pulls up along the curb in front of Mrs. O'Leary's house. Three young men hop out, all bundled up in Carhartt overalls and coats. While almost unrecognizable under their winter gear, they must be Rick, Steve, and Nate. Rick and Steve instantly go to the rear of the house to Mrs. O'Leary's garage. Nate, the oldest and, I believe, graduating high school this spring, rummages around the back seat as I finish. I'm anxious to check on Frost. Nate begins to head my way.

"Hey Dana!" he shouts. "Grandma said you found a cat and would need a starter kit. My mom put a few things together for you."

He offers a reusable tote bag full of food, treats, toys and miscellaneous items that, as a non-cat owner, I am not privy to, along with a box that has a bed, litter box and litter. I'm truly blown away. I try to utter a thank you, but Nate shuts me down instantly with a wave of his hand. "Mom says thank you for making her get rid of it all. "

I take the bag from him and gesture for him to follow me to the side of the house. "I am so appreciative. I don't know how to care for a cat. You don't know anyone missing one or who is looking to adopt a friendly feline do you?"

"No, I don't but I'll ask around."

I motion for Nate to drop the box on the steps. "You tell your mom if she ever needs something I can help with, to just say the word"

Nate chuckles. "According to Dad, taking all this stuff was enough. Good luck with your new fur baby. I have to go help my brothers with Grandma's house. See ya later, Dana."

"Bye, Nate."

I put the shovel away then drop the items Nate gave me in the mudroom. I venture a peek at my visitor. She has changed positions but is still mostly wrapped up. There is a tiny tug at my heartstrings. She is so sweet. I haul the cat supplies to where Frost is resting to take stock.

The litter box and food are probably the most urgent to get put together. I have no idea how much litter to put in the bottom of this plastic box, nor do I know when to change it, so I grab my phone and start researching. The bag is huge and, judging from what I am reading, it should be able to fill the box twice. I need to use the slotted shovel I found in the bag between changes. The mudroom seems like the best place for this. There is a partially used bag of kibble. Do they even call cat food kibble? I sprinkle a bit in a small bowl and put it next to the water dish. Hopefully, I am doing this right.

Frost stirs. Gently scooping her under her ribs, I try to investigate a bit more so I know what to mention to the vet when I call. We meander into the mudroom, and I deposit her onto the litter. I have no idea if she knows what to do, but I need her to know where to do it. She scratches and squats. Interesting. This makes me think she must be someone's pet.

Leaving her to do her business, I wander out to the kitchen. Time to call the veterinarian. The beauty of small towns is that nothing goes unnoticed and since there is only one vet in town, he will surely know who owns this sweet fur ball.

The phone is picked up on the second ring. "Good morning. Sheyenne Valley Vet, Maren speaking. How can I help you?"

"Maren, this is Dana Dodds. How are you this chilly morning?"

"Dana, it's good to hear from you. Lots of rescheduling this morning, it's just too cold to be out. I hear you have a kitty. Is that why you are calling?"

I chuckle. "It never fails to surprise me how fast news travels in this town. That's exactly why I am calling. I found her stowed away in my garage and there may be frostbite damage to one ear. I am no expert so I would like Dr. Davis to take a look at her. I am also wondering if anyone is missing a little gray fluff ball."

I haven't heard of anyone missing a cat. Maybe she has a microchip. Can you bring her in at 10:30 and we'll check her out?"

"I can and will. Thanks, Maren."

We say our goodbyes and I look down. Frost has found the water dish. She doesn't seem interested in the food, but she is definitely drinking and starting to explore her surroundings. She is adorable and quickly worming her way into my heart.

We have over an hour before we have to go out into the frozen tundra and she seems content in my home, wandering around and rolling on the rug. I put out the cat bed, add the towels she was wrapped in, pour another cup of coffee and amble down the hall to the bathroom to clean up.

Keeping the door open a crack so that we can keep an eye on each other, I de-layer myself, pile my hair on top of my head and jump in the shower. While I'm drying off, Frost pokes her little face into the bathroom. I'm curious as to how old she may be.

I hurry through my routine of moisturizing then decide that I shouldn't need as many layers for just a dash to the car and building. Jeans and a hoodie should do. I run a brush through my hair and decide that the braid is, once again, the way to go.

Frost rubs against my calves and feet, her little motor running loudly. I lean down and give her a scratch and am rewarded by a face rub against my hand.

"You are the sweetest little thing! There's time for another cup of coffee and some snuggles if you are up for it? I know I am."

I take my mug to the coffee maker and doctor another dose of creamer with coffee before depositing myself on the couch. Frost joins me instantly, standing on my lap and chest and kneading at me with her little engine running full bore. I think she likes me. After a few seconds, she settles across my chest and stomach and drops off to sleep.

All too soon it is time to get moving. Boots on, jacket on, keys in hand, I dash to the garage and car. Wrestling the garage door open, I click the battery-operated locks on my key fob. It is so cold that the metal of the car door groans as I open it. I slide into a driver's seat like a block of ice--hard, solid, and cold. The engine turns over a couple times before it fires and catches. Once the car is idling, I sprint to the house and am met by a blast of heat, reminding me just how darn cold it is. My lungs sting from the sprint and my fingers tingle from touching the metal of the car and the garage door, but I wasn't out in the elements long enough for concern.

I stride into the living room to check on Frost. She raises her head and lets out a little "mew". She is quickly growing on me and a little part of me is hoping I can keep her.

"Are you up for this sweetheart?" I say, sitting down next to her. "We're going to go meet Dr. Davis. He is very nice and not bad looking. I think he's going to like you as much as I do."

I give her a few scratches and her purr kicks in right away. "You're just glad to be warm, loved and inside, aren't you, baby?"

My wallet tucked into the inside pocket of my coat, all my gear on, I scoop my little girl into the warmth of my layers and zip up around the tiny little body. The car is warming nicely although a bit on the stiff side still.--Days like these make me promise myself to get an automatic garage door opener and I will undoubtedly say that same thing on the next icicle of a day.

Sheyenne Valley Veterinary sits in the heart of town, a stone's throw from the police station and city hall. Its stone-carved facade was originally built to house a long since defunct Elk's lodge The carved elks' heads, buntings and fleurs add an odd charm to the building. Snowplows have been out and a crew has already cleared walks. I take a front spot and peer down through my scarf to see how Frost is doing. I do believe she is asleep again. I prepare myself for the onslaught of biting air and push open the door. There is the hint of a breeze, and it makes the air temperature feel so much harsher. With gloved hands, I wrench open the frosted glass door and I'm enveloped in warmth once again.

"Hi Dana!" the friendly Maren exclaims. "Where is your new friend?"

I tug off my mittens, unwind the scarf from my head. "Good morning, Maren. Thanks for getting me in on such short notice."

"Oh, don't mention it. Almost every appointment before noon cancelled so making time was easy. Oh! Would you look at her!", she says as I extricate Frost from the depths of my coat. "She's so small. I wonder how old she is. May I?" She stretches out her arms.

Taking the kitten, she says, "I see what you mean about the ear but to the naked eye, the rest of her looks fine. Let's get you both into an exam room and I'll get Doc."

Maren leads us to a small room with a stainless-steel table in the center, a sink and some cabinetry along the wall. Posters on the wall tell me not to feed my pet people food and warn me about wood ticks and Lyme disease. She hands Frost to me and lets me know Dr. Davis will be with me soon, then darts off to answer a ringing phone.

I haven't been in this office since just after Mom passed away and her beloved beagle Buddy became ill. Dr. Davis and his staff were with me during the process of euthanizing him. A very tough day, but I had some solace knowing he was with Mom again, and the clinic was so wonderful to me.

Mere minutes later, the door on the other side of the room opens. Dr. Mark Davis is in his mid-50's and has been the town vet for what seems like eons. Everyone adores him and since that day with Buddy, I have seen him around town at ball games, charity benefits, and occasionally we pass on the bike path or at the grocery. I wouldn't call us friends but certainly acquaintances.

Dr. Davis has been a widower for over 10 years, having lost his wife Elizabeth to cancer around the same time Mom and I lost Dad. A few months after that, Mom decided to move here, to her hometown. The Davis' had two young children at the time. Now, Jesse has just started college and Anna will graduate high school in another year or so. Every divorcee in town thinks Dr. Davis is a hot commodity. From previous interactions I've had with him, he seems like a very kind and caring person. He isn't too hard on the eyes either, if you don't mind the tall athletic type.

"Dana." He smiles. "How have you been? Maren tells me you found a cat."

I unfold my arms to show him Frost. "I did. She was hiding in the garage. From the looks of it, she was out in the snow last night and managed to wedge herself under some broken weather stripping. I found her nestled into my patio cushions, trying to get warm. She was frozen pretty solid when I found her. Her fur had been wet at some point and she was all iced over. I took her inside right away and noticed the damage to the one ear. I did investigate and didn't see anything else, but I don't know what I am looking for. I hope she has a microchip so I can return her to her owner. Someone must be worried."

Dr. Davis motions for me to place Frost on the table. He investigates her tiny frame. She suddenly looks much smaller against man-sized hands. "The only sign of damage I see is the tip of her left ear. You did a good job of warming her up and caring for her. She seems to be rebounding nicely."

He listens to her heart, feels her ribs and stomach, looks in her ear, eyes, and even her nose, mumbling updates the entire time -- probably more for himself than me. He takes an instrument out of a drawer, turns it on, and passes it over her body.

"No chip." He sighs. "It looks like you may be the proud owner of a cat. No one has called to say they are missing one. You could put a call in to Joe Darnell over at the police station to see if anyone has talked to him."

"Dr. Davis-"

"Please, call me Mark," he interjects, smiling.

"Mark, I don't know the first thing about cats. I don't know how old she is"

"3 to 4 months, give or take."

"I don't know what they eat."

"Maren can help you with that up front when you leave. We have some options, or you can pick up kibble made especially for kittens anywhere in town."

"Can she be left alone? Do I kennel her? I don't know how to cat." I throw my hands up in the air.

He laughs, patting my forearm. "Dana, relax. She will let you know what she needs. If you know someone who has a cat, have them come over and answer your questions. If you don't find someone to take her and her owner doesn't come forward, there is a shelter about an hour away in Hermantown. Otherwise, she still has her claws, and I would recommend a good scratching post or you are likely to end up needing new furniture. I should check out her ear in 2 weeks. I will send you home with antibiotics, but some cats can be a challenge when it comes time to take them."

I feel the color drain from my face. "I'm not a cat person."

"She doesn't know that," he whispers, handing Frost to me. "Besides, you are good with animals. You were fabulous with Buddy and that dog was stubborn. What will you name her?"

"I have been calling her Frost."

Dr. Davis - Mark - chuckles "If you've named her, she already has your heart. Can you think of any other questions for me?"

"Yes. Are you going to stop by and make sure I'm not screwing this up?" My words drip with sarcasm.

"You won't screw it up, but if you need me, just call. I can make myself available," he assures me, then walks us out to Maren's desk. He gives her some instructions regarding follow up appointments and, with a quick squeeze to my shoulder, tells me someone will have my antibiotic out in a few minutes. I feel a little lost. While yes, she is a sweet kitten, I didn't want a kitten. I had hoped she would have a chip and a panicked owner.

Dr. Davis seems far more friendly than I remember him. I'm not sure what to make of the squeeze and his comment about being available if I need him. That seems to be going above and beyond the normal patient to vet protocol. While being on more personal terms would be pleasant, I will stick to being professional. At least for now.

I make my follow up appointments. Maren helps me choose a food that is specifically designed for kittens, reminds me I can call the office for anything, and there are no silly questions. While we wait for the prescription, Maren phones Joe at the police station. She confirms he hasn't taken any calls for a missing cat and gives him my contact information should someone claim her. A tech comes out with a small bag containing a bottle of pills and directions. She also gives me explicit details on how to get Frost to take them, along with some options. Feeling a bit overwhelmed, I place Frost into my jacket and we dash out to the car.

The drive home is a quiet one. Maybe I can find someone to take her. Would I be able to give her away? Where will she sleep? How big will she get? What if I suck at being a cat lady? Or what if I become the crazy cat lady all the kids talk about? People leave cats alone in their house, don't they? Do people walk cats? I have so many questions and feel so unprepared.

I pull into the driveway, park, and, with cat-in-coat, head inside. I lightly plonk Frost onto the floor. She promptly issues a loud 'meow' and I laugh.

"Well, little girl, looks like you are going to be here for a bit. Let's get some things in place and figure out what you need. First, let's move the water bowl and food dish into the kitchen. C'mon," I say as I pick up the bowls and walk towards the kitchen. Frost gets very friendly and courageously tries to wind between my legs. It is a challenge not to step on her. Giggling at her, I put the bowls down against the side of the refrigerator.

"Let's go grab the bag of food we got at the vet's office and see if you will eat that."

Frost mews in response. Together we pour the old food into the bag it came from, and tear open this new one. She purrs like crazy and rubs herself all over me and the bag so that it is hard to get anything done.

"Silly girl." I laugh while pouring. "Let's see if you will eat this one."

Frost attacks the bowl with a frenzy. She was hungry! She pauses and rubs her face across my hand and calf before refocusing her energy on the bowl. I put the bag of cat food into the bag from Mrs. O'Leary's daughter and sprinkle a few toys on the floor. How do cats play?

My thoughts are interrupted by the doorbell. I can see Mike Miller's mail truck parked out front.

"Hi, Mike. Did I order something and then forget?" I say, joking.

"Ha! Not this time Dana." He hands over a brown paper bag. "Connie heard you got a surprise cat and thought she would send over some things to help you get started. There are some pill pockets in there, but they don't always work. Sometimes you have to hide their medicine in some canned cat food. She has a couple cans of that in there too, along with a loaf of her famous banana bread."

"Oh my gosh! Thank you! Thank Connie for me. This is so very kind of you. Completely unexpected. Does everyone know I found a stray?"

Mike grins from ear to ear. "Our son's fiancé works with Dr. Davis, so we got the inside scoop." He lets out a little laugh. "She didn't call to spread gossip as much as to see if we knew who the little critter could belong to. Oh, look at her! She is so small."

Frost had made her way into the entry to inspect our guest.

I scoop her up. "Hey girl, you have your first visitor. Mike, this is Frost. Frost, this is our friend Mike."

Mike reaches out to rub her head but hesitates when he sees the curling ear. Instead, he caresses her chin and neck, and is rewarded with a loud purr.

Mike lets out another laugh. "She sure is a happy one. She will fit right in here."

"In all honesty, I had hoped she would be chipped, and I would be able to find someone who was missing her. I have never had a cat and don't quite know what to do with her."

"Ah, you'll be fine. Cats need love and to be left alone. They will let you know which one they need. But I'd better get to my route." He gives the purring kitten one more rub. "You two have a good day. And you," he wags a finger at Frost, "stay inside now, you hear?" A quick wave and he is down the steps and off in the truck.

I place Frost on the floor, then carry the newly acquired treasures into the kitchen. Sure enough, there are soft little things to hide pills in, a half dozen cans of wet food, a container of treats, a little pink collar with a bell, and a loaf of banana bread. Connie's banana bread is all the rage at bake sales. I am secretly hoping it is one with miniature chocolate chips in it. I peel the foil open and instantly spot chocolate. On days when small town life grates on my nerves, I'll remember this day.

I sneak a peek into the living room and find Frost curled up on the rug, basking in a sunbeam. Perfectly comfortable. I take out a frozen serving of homemade chicken wild rice soup and plop it into the microwave. After a few short minutes during which I rearranged the pantry to make room for my new roommate's stash, the microwave alerts me that it is time to eat. Grabbing a towel to help carry the hot bowl to the kitchen island, I pull up a stool.

While I wait for my soup to cool, I read the directions on the antibiotics. One tablet every 24 hours and they are actually pretty large. She should be able to swallow them, but will she? I screw the lid on and pick up my spoon. Maybe between supper and bed would be the best time for this.

After cleaning up the kitchen, I wander past Frost sitting on the windowsill and down the hall to my office. I was lucky enough to be working for a large accounting firm when Mom got sick a few years ago. Management adapted my position to make it easier for me to move in here and take care of her. After she passed, I didn't want to leave this delightful town filled with kind, generous, albeit nosy people and the firm agreed to keep me employed remotely.

I flip open my laptop and decide to answer as many emails as I can. Frost is mewing down the hall so I holler, "Silly girl, I'm right here." She enters the office and tries to hop up onto my lap. I give her a hand and once in my lap, she curls right up and naps again. Getting work done today shouldn't be too hard.

Around 5 p.m. I shut down the laptop. Frost has moved to the corner of my desk and has been batting at my pen while I write. I can't decide if this is cute or annoying, but it does make me smile.

"Alright, little girl, we are done in here for the day," I say as I head out of the room. She hops onto the chair, then to the floor, and goes directly to the laundry room. Part of me wants to follow to see what she is doing and the other part of me is certain I don't need to check on her bathroom abilities. The 'follow' part of me wins. I pick up the towels she was wrapped in that morning and tag along. As I drop them in the basket, I see her doing exactly what I suspected she would, and I leave.

I think about giving her the pill and if it doesn't work, I can add it to a little of the canned food and call it her supper. I fish out one of the pill pockets and read the directions. *Place pill inside and seal around it*. This shouldn't be hard but now that it is encased in this treat it looks even bigger.

I get down on the floor when Frost head my way and call her to me. Once in my lap, I show her the treat. She sniffs it and gives me a look. She knows I am trying to pull a fast one.

"Do you want a treat? It's nummy. Look." I try to make eye contact while pretending to eat it. I am definitely going to be the crazy lady the kids will talk about.

She is unimpressed and turns away. This isn't going to work. I get out a small bowl and open a can of wet food that smells awful. Dismantling the useless pill pocket, I dig out the antibiotic, find a rather large chunk of meat in the food to try to camouflage the pill, add some of the kibble to the bowl with half the can, and stir a bit. Maybe she won't notice something hard if there are other solid items mixed in. She can smell the food and is wrapping around my legs quite aggressively. This could work.

Positioning the bowl, I say, "I can see you are hungry. Let's hope you like this."

While she is having her dinner, I assemble a salad. By the time I am ready to eat, Frost is finished and has walked away from the bowl. There, in the center, is the bright orange pill. Dammit. How did she know?

I finish my salad while researching videos on 'How to Give a Cat a Pill'. Frost is on the floor playing, without a care in the world. I watch another video. I'm going to have to hold her, pry open her mouth, poke the pill so far back into her mouth that she can't spit it out, then rub her throat to help her swallow it. A sense of dread solidifies. I wish she would have just eaten it with the food.

I pick the now-dry pill out of the bowl, carry it and a glass of water into the living room to watch TV until I have the guts to manhandle her.

I watch one more video in an attempt to find the courage or confidence for the task at hand, but it's time to stop procrastinating. I try to position my fingers on either side of her jaw and she immediately fights; head and paws swing, scratching both my arms and howling. She manages to bite me as I shove the pill into her, but I rub her throat for a few minutes. I hold the water glass out to her, she sniffs, then drinks. A success even though both my arms are bleeding. I give her a hug, telling her what a good girl she is.

In the kitchen, I wash up my arms to clean the scratches, take the pink collar out to the living room and shake the little bell for her. Nonplussed, she ignores me. Not long after, she begins retching and throws up orange slime. My success is short-lived. On my hands and knees with paper towels and spray cleaner, I tell her it's not her fault, that I am not mad. At least she missed the rug. The wood floor is far easier to clean. I take the used supplies to the garbage, wash up again, and settle in on the couch for the remainder of the evening while I contemplate my next move.

I'll call Dr. Davis's office in the morning. Maybe the antibiotic comes in a liquid. Maybe they have a tip or trick to help. Clearly, I need something. In the meantime, I have to figure out bedtime. I feel more comfortable knowing where she is, so I will close her in with me. I drop the cat bed next to mine and flip on the bathroom light. While I wash my face and brush my teeth, she bats at the running water. Having a cat is enough, I don't need a wet one.

Once finished, I drop her onto the bed and climb under the covers. She immediately climbs to my chest, front paws kneading at my collar bone, rear feet stabbing at my intestines or spleen. How do people do this? Thankfully, she drops to her belly and the purring begins. She's hot and loud. What have I gotten myself into?

I eventually drift off to sleep, only to wake with a desire to roll onto my side, but I am trapped under an engine block. I try to shimmy out from under Frost, only to rouse her and have her stand on all my internal organs. How does something so small hurt so much? I give her a little nudge, and I quickly roll to where I am comfortable. She paces a bit and curls up in a ball behind my knees. Any hope of further rolling has now been dashed. I drift off again.

I wake to filtered sunlight and silence. Where is Frost? Why can't I hear her? I sit up in bed. She has to be in this room. The door is shut. As I look at the window, the shape of a feline is silhouetted on the blinds. She is enjoying the morning sun. I haven't inadvertently killed my new kitten--yet.

I throw off the covers and hop out of bed. A tiny face peeks at me from around the corner of the blinds.

"Good morning, Frost. How did you sleep?" She joins me in the bathroom, winding around my legs. "I would bet you are hungry, aren't you?"

I put on my robe, head to the kitchen, and open the pantry for the bag of cat food. I take down a clean bowl and add the allotted amount as per the directions on the bag. Frost is meowing with vigor.

"You aren't starving, you know? You have had a couple meals here now. I won't let you go hungry."

I check the time on the microwave. Two hours until the veterinarian's office opens.

I curl up on the couch to sip my coffee and turn on the television. The meteorologist confirms what I had surmised. It is -17 F. Still dangerously cold. Thank goodness I work from home.

Frost hops up onto the couch and climbs me. She stands on my chest, pressing her forehead against my chin. I give her a smooch. She mews and repeats. It seems we have a game. We continue the kiss and nudge, while watching the weather report for the next few days. This cold snap is due to lighten up but not for a bit.

I take Frost's collar with the bell and fasten it around her neck. She doesn't seem to mind it. I throw on a short-sleeved sweater and jeans and check the scratches on my arms. They are scabbed over but not red, so I am not concerned about infection.

At 8 a.m. I take my phone off the charger and make the call. Maren's chipper voice greets me. "Good morning, Sheyenne Valley Vet, Maren speaking. How can I help you?"

"Maren, It's Dana Dodds again."

"Hi, Dana. Is everything ok with your kitten?"

"I guess so. I am having some difficulties with the antibiotics." I inform her of the different methods I employed and how she rewarded me by throwing up the pill. I ask her if there is something else I can do, or if they come in a liquid form. She takes notes and tells me someone will get back to me soon. I say thanks and head down the hall to the office with Frost in tow.

After a few hours, my phone rings. The caller ID tells me it is Dr. Davis' office.

"Hi, Dana. It's Maren returning your call. I spoke to the tech and we decided that one of us will drop by on our way home from work today to see if we can help you."

"Oh my gosh! That is so much more than I expected. Are you sure? I can bring her in."

"Doc says not to bring her out again. Watch for one of us to pop in around 5:30".

"I am beyond grateful. Thank you so much!"

"It's no problem, Dana. We're happy to help. See you soon."

I check the time. It is almost noon and time for a much-needed break. Frost has been in and out of the room all morning and, judging from the placement of toys, has played a bit. I check the litter box, scoop it clean with the little shovel and deposit the bag in the garbage can in my garage. It is still bitterly cold. I shiver as I close the door again.

Washing my hands, I check Frost's bowl and there is still food in it, so she is good. Unloading more of the items previously prepared for salads from the fridge, I assemble another and take a stool at the counter. Trying to climb my jeans with her little claws, Frost is attempting to reach the counter. I remove her and deposit her to the floor.

"Sorry, sweetie. You don't belong up here, especially when someone is eating."

I clean up my mess, announcing to Frost that I have a few more hours of work to do. The bell on her collar tinkles down the hall behind me. In no time she is sprawled across my keyboard making it very difficult to get anything done. I can't decide if this is adorable or exasperating, but either way it causes me to laugh.

"You know, I didn't want a cat, but you have made me smile more in thirty-six hours than I thought possible. Maybe my life was missing something."

My afternoon flies by and pretty soon I can log off and call it a day. I shut everything down and move Frost's bed to my room. Someone from the vet's office should be here soon so I do a ten second tidy. I find a small wicker basket to use for all the new cat toys spread around my living room and a small noisy ball goes whizzing past me. I chuckle, flick it, and watch her pounce.

A little bit later the doorbell rings and Frost races to the front door.

"Let me get the door open, baby" I say, nudging her out of the way.

I open the door to Dr. Davis, himself, and usher him in out of the cold. "Dr. Davis, I am so sorry to impose on your time like this. I had thought Maren would drop by."

"It's no problem. Both Maren and Olivia offered to stop by, but I had nothing planned. This way they can go home to their families. Hello, Frost," he says grinning while she winds around his legs. "Besides, you did tell me I should stop in and check to make sure you weren't screwing things up, didn't you?"

"Come in, come in," I add, retreating further and making room. "And, yes, I did. I was being facetious though." His visit is unexpected and will surely have the neighbors talking. I smile just thinking about the stories that will undoubtedly make their way around to me.

"Your arms." He takes my wrist for a closer look. His touch is light and sweet, and I find myself a little nervous, like a 16-year-old on a first date.

"Oh, it isn't so bad. They're already scabbed over."

"Is this from trying to get her to take a pill?"

"It is. She was not impressed with me." I laugh.

Handing me the bag, he replies, "Well, now I'm glad I picked this up on my way. You need a break."

I can see a bottle of wine and the makings of a charcuterie board inside the bag. I suddenly feel my face flush. Is this a house call, friendly visit, or some kind of date? I find myself excitedly hoping for the latter. "This is very nice, Dr. Davis, but not necessary."

"Nonsense, and I thought we agreed on Mark."

"Mark," I parrot.

"Better. Thank you."

"I can imagine the gossip that is already spreading about the most eligible bachelor in town showing up at my house with wine and cheese."

Mark gathers Frost and follows me into the kitchen. I get down a board and some small bowls while he examines his patient. I assemble the board, the makings of which have come from The Urban Olive, one of my favorite places to stop for dinner. I take two wine glasses out and pull an opener from a drawer. Mark takes them from me and proceeds to expertly open the wine.

"Jake over at the liquor store said you like reds, so I hope this one is alright. It's one of my favorites. What?"

I realize my cheeks are burning. "You asked Jake what I drink, and ordered for two from Urban? You realize half the town is waiting to see just how long your car sits at my curb and I'm now the enemy of every divorced woman in town? By morning, we will be bigger news than that house fire."

"For starters, I didn't realize I was such a prize. That explains why some of the women in town bring me their pets for every little thing. If I had known, I may have been more discreet but probably not. Let them talk. This town needs a little action. Let's take a look at your kitten while the wine breathes."

I retell the events from last night, showing him the pill pocket and the canned food. I finish with the cleaning of the floor story. My nervousness dissipates and I am surprised at how easy he is to talk to and how his presence in my home is comfortable.

"Do you have a very sharp knife, razor blade, or pill cutter?" he asks.

"Oh, I hadn't thought to cut them in half. Do you think it will make a difference? I have a pill cutter in the hall closet"

"Can't hurt to try."

I return with the cutter and dump one pill into my hand, then proceed to chop it in half.

"Let's skip the pockets since she turned up her nose at them. I like what you did with the wet food, so try that again. Bury both halves of the pill in it and let's see what happens."

"Sounds good." I retrieve a small plate and grab the half-empty can of food from the previous night. I smoosh the halves into chunks of meat and I stir in a bit of the kibble.

"This smells awful, but she certainly doesn't think so."

Frost meows loudly and aggressively smashes her head against my calves. As soon as the plate hits the floor, she is all over it.

"About how long after you got the pill into her last night did she vomit?"

"Maybe a half hour or forty minutes. Why?"

"I want to stick around that long to see if it happens again. I don't think they are too harsh for her stomach, but I can't always be certain."

"Mmm, makes sense. How about I grab a couple of plates while you pour?"

Mark pours the perfect portion of wine in each glass and makes himself at home on a stool while I get forks, plates, and napkins. I arrange the items on the island and take the stool next to him. He has picked a position where he can keep an eye on my girl. He glances at her frequently.

We each dish up items from the charcuterie board while making small talk about Urban Olive, our favorite wines, and this awful cold snap. Frost finishes eating and has seemingly ingested the halves of the pill in the process.

While I put the remnants of the board in the fridge, Mark pours each of us a second glass of wine. I pick mine up and motion for him to follow me into the living room. I curl into my usual corner of the couch and he takes the other end. Frost is sprawled across the cushion between us and seems content to be the focus of attention.

I don't know much about this man except for what I have heard around town. I didn't realize he takes his kids skiing in Montana every year or that he had started the tradition shortly after Elizabeth's death. He tells me a little about each child, beaming with pride the entire time. We talk about Mom, the updates I have made to her old house to make it a little more mine, and places we have traveled or would like to. Our conversation has an easy flow and I feel like I know so much more about him.

"It is getting late, and I think I have sufficiently given the town something to talk about. Frost has managed to keep her meds down, so I had better get going."

"I am a bit embarrassed that I didn't think to cut the pill. I wondered if they were too big."

"No need to be embarrassed. It was the perfect opportunity for me to get to know you a little."

"This was nice. Bringing dinner was a nice touch", I add, walking him to the door.

He slips his shoes on and gathers up his jacket. "Would you be interested in doing this again? Maybe we can go out to dinner and really give the town something to talk about?"

Trying to keep my cool, I raise an eyebrow. "That could prove to be fun."

"Great. Consider it a date."

I have an official date with the town's most eligible bachelor. Inside I am squealing like a teenager.

He runs a finger down my jaw and my stomach does a little flip. I suddenly hope he kisses me. I really want him to kiss me.

"Are you ok with people talking about us? Because they will."

"I am guessing there were tongues wagging before the door shut behind you at the liquor store this afternoon."

The corners of his eyes crinkle. "You are probably right".

He locks eyes with me for a moment or two as if testing me, takes my hand, then slowly leans in and gives me the tenderest of kisses. Instant butterflies. My insides have turned to mush and I don't think my legs work.

"I'll call you, ok?"

I nod, suddenly unable to find my voice.

"Good night, Dana." He leaves, closing the door behind him in a rush of cold air.

"Well, little one", I exclaim, picking up Frost. "I believe I need to say thanks. Because of you, I have a date with the good doctor. You planned it that way, didn't you?"

-- S.Y. Quinn writes everything from poems to short stories, romance to humor. She is a long-time member of the Moorhead Friends Writing Group and has lived in the Fargo Moorhead area for over 30 years. While she does not have a slew of published works, she can claim ownership of *Stronger* published by the Potato Soup Journal. Ms. Quinn maintains a busy lifestyle that includes working for an international nonprofit and a local bookstore along with researching an upcoming book idea and volunteering at a local dog rescue.

For Every Action

By Alexander Vayle

Ten miles from town. That was how far Aaron Brandler estimated they'd gone after he'd chased the man from Heather's apartment, pursued him in his Chevy, and finally lost control when a sharp turn sent both their vehicles sliding into the ditch. Then he climbed out of the tilted truck, scrambled down, and pursued again.

The snow made it difficult, but rage fueled him. He charged through rippling drifts in the open field—lungs on fire and legs hot with blood—kicking the deep fluff into clouds.

The wind made the chase harder still. A constant spray of fine, crystallized snow felt like being blasted by sand. He closed his eyes against it, peeking intermittently to keep a bead on his target, not twenty yards ahead.

There were hills nearby, rolling and easily farmed. Near the river, in the direction of the pursuit, was a different story entirely. The land sank sharply. The hillsides which led to the river's edge were more akin to cliffs; steep and rough-skinned with rocks and old snapped-off roots to tear at clothes and flesh.

The man approached the broken edge of land and Aaron shouted a warning for him to stop. He looked back. Four rough lines on his cheek were a flash of red against the muted colors of winter. When he faced forward again, Aaron saw his immediate attempt to halt.

Not from around here, Aaron thought. *It's gotta be Casey. Everyone around here knows the drop-offs.* And everyone did. Everyone local, that was. Those who lived, worked, and raised their kids in and around Fenton knew the tale of the Bratten boy who launched his four-wheeler over the edge and was found twenty feet below with a broken neck. Much speculation was offered among the old farmers as to whether he would have lived if he hadn't tried to stop. "Little more speed, he'da hit the river. Still be alive today." "How old would that boy be now?" "Well, let's see." But he had slowed down. Just like the man Aaron chased.

The blanket of snow was thinner near the edge—to the calves instead of the thighs—and the man had gathered speed. If he'd maintained such speed, the momentum would have arched his path into the air. Though still a fall of twenty-odd feet, he'd have landed in a massive drift that ran along the western shore of the river—something to the tune of six feet deep.

Instead, when the man seemed to recognize what the blinding snow had concealed, he put on the brakes, skidded a foot or two, and toppled forward with his arms spinning uselessly in the air. The man disappeared from Aaron's sight. A second later cries of pain broke through the wind as the man grated down the wall of the ravine.

By the time Aaron made the edge, there was silence. He approached with caution and peered over. The man had scraped his way down outcroppings of rock and the fall seemed to terminate on the root ball of a dead tree. A short distance from the tree, the man was slowly limping away, like an animal who'd been struck by a car.

No coat. No hat. The man had no time to collect them before he fled the apartment. He struggled through the wide drift along the shore; crawling over a couple feet, sinking in, and digging his way back up. Fresh blood matted his dirty-blond hair and ran down his neck. A trail of blood, that seemed to emanate from beneath him, lay in his wake. The man laid his head down on the drift and pulled in a few huge, panting breaths, then started forward again.

Aaron's jaw clenched and his fists locked into weapons as frustration added to his anger. He was supposed to be the one to deliver these blows. Not a stone. Nature held no feeling for Heather. Its justice was indifferent. As perhaps justice should be. But not this day. This day punishment was supposed to be lashed out. An eye for an eye. Pain for pain until the seething flood of loss and wrath inside him was poured over this man.

Ideas sped by. *Leave him down there to die. No, better yet, go down there and kick his ass. He's too hurt to fight, it'd be easy as…as what? As fighting a man who's injured, I guess. Probably like fighting a little kid.* The shame of his own thoughts began to wave down his rage. When he closed his eyes and imagined beating a man as he crawled along the ground, he felt sick. The act was nothing of him, it was born of hate, and—time unknown—it would pass.

Aaron's teeth stopped grinding. His fists loosened. He would confront, capture if necessary. Call the police and EMS, but only after he had time alone with this man. If robbed of justice, he would at least be the one to receive the answer to the only question which mattered, "Why?"

Aaron took his time on the slope, eyeing it out first and spotting a usable root here, a foothold there. He was in shape, near his prime, and the climb went with ease. As he descended, he found the straight winds passed overhead, but within the ravine was a relative calm.

Once safely to the bottom, the root ball caught his eye. One root in particular, a couple inches in diameter, struck straight up and appeared freshly broken off at the end. *The broken-off piece is in his guts,* he thought. He was right.

Cutting through the bank was easier for Aaron. A path of sorts already existed. Still, it took him a few minutes to reach the other side where the snow tapered down near the river's edge.

The man had made it out onto the ice and collapsed. He lay on his side, breathing hard. One arm out-stretched, as if considering whether it was worth the effort to pull himself a bit further. One hand guarded his abdomen. A crimson smear was freezing on the ice behind him, and more blood leaked between his fingers. He didn't look up as Aaron slowly approached and stood over him.

"You're Casey, aren't you? Heather...Heather's ex?"

No answer.

"Why'd ya do it? That's all I want to know. Why?"

Casey took a moment, eyes distant. "I didn't mean...to kill her."

Aaron didn't believe him, and didn't respond.

"I'm always pissed off...can't control it. I'm like...my dad, I guess. Always pissed."

Aaron knelt, anger beginning to simmer once more, and locked onto his eyes. "You don't get to make an excuse."

Casey turned his face to Aaron.

"Yeah? What about you? What excuse...do you have? Heather was my girlfriend. Not an ex. Think I don't know what you were doing there? I'm not…stupid. She was cheating on me with you. I've loved her since we were kids and she wanted to dump me…because of *you*." He closed his eyes as his face grew taught and pained.

Aaron looked away for a moment. He was guilty, to some degree at least. Heather moved to town, into her first apartment, almost a month prior. She and Aaron met and connected instantly. There hadn't been sex. Not yet. Aaron never even had the pleasure of calling her his girlfriend. Or introducing her to his parents, his friends. It all came crashing down because of the man bleeding out onto the ice in front of him.

Aaron glared at Casey, but he was seeing Heather's apartment. Not an hour had passed since he'd showed up with wine purchased by an older sister and dropped it to the floor with a meaningless *cunk* when he found the door standing open and a streak of blood on the white wall.

The attack should never have happened. The physical distance between Heather and Casey should have been the final blow to the failing relationship. Yet it lingered, held together by Heather's fear of what Casey would do if she ended it. A justified fear, as it turned out.

"You should have let her go." Aaron said.

"And you shouldn'ta slept with my girlfriend."

"I *didn't*."

"Liar."

Aaron wanted to retort, but he knew the words were useless. An argument to the end of time wouldn't change a thing.

He eyed Casey's wound. Casey followed his gaze, lifted his hand, and saw the blood flow bright and steady, then quickly resumed pressure on his wound.

The man Casey was becoming gave way to the youth he hadn't yet outgrown. His breath sped, mouth grew taught, eyes glistened. He scanned around, as if to confirm the ugliness of the situation the two of them were in.

"I fell hard. *Really* hard. It's…it's…"

"Bad."

"I'm gonna die, right?"

Aaron didn't answer; an answer in itself.

"Oh shit, oh shit, oh jeez man. You gotta call…an ambulance. You gotta call. I'm sorry, okay? I'm sorry man. I'm sorry, I'm sorry, I'm—"

Casey wept. Swore. Peeked at his belly again. Wept and cursed and begged some more.

Aaron, on the surface, remained stoic. Beneath the facade, he was remembering blood. An arterial gush when his uncle slaughtered hogs. His first dog, laying in long grass and dripping with gore, after fighting his way out of a tangle of barbed wire. Aaron was wondering how much blood Casey had lost so far, how much more he could. Lastly, or perhaps behind it all, he was seeing Heather as he found her in the bedroom, stone still and awkwardly sprawled over a stack of boxes. Red trenches carved down her bare back and the handle of a knife sticking out.

Anger came and Aaron grew hot with it. He'd momentarily closed his eyes to view the past. However, when he opened them, ready to strike, he saw a whimpering, bleeding man laying in front of him. No, not a man anymore. A weakling kid. An easier target for pity than anger. A voice, sounding much like his dad, spoke in Aaron's head: *Do the right thing, kid.*

Aaron doffed his gloves and stuffed them in his pockets. He pulled out his phone and swiped the screen. His thumb felt the cracks at the same time his eyes registered the shattered glass.

"Oh shit." Aaron recalled the accident. Watching Casey's car take the turn, slide, go in. Trying to break, the helpless feeling of having no control for the few seconds when it mattered most. Then hitting the ditch, getting knocked into the passenger's seat, his leg slamming into the gear shift on the way.

"I…I can't call. I really can't." He flipped his phone over to show Casey.

Casey wiped away tears with his forearm and stared at the phone. His sobs subsided as his demeanor turned to a blank stun. Eventually, his gaze floated up to Aaron and the men shared a speechless moment of understanding.

Casey rolled to his back and viewed the distant sky. Aaron was caught between a desire to comfort the dying and the desire to gloat at the wondrous inevitability of Karma. Mid-debate, Casey had shifted his gaze to the tree whose roots had delivered the fatal blow. The upper half of the tree had fallen over the river long ago and was stripped of bark. Where a cluster of branches were frozen in, the ice looked weak. Liquid water ringed each wooden arm.

Casey seemed to calm as he gazed at it. Aaron remained quiet, wondering what Casey was thinking. Finally, Casey said, "My mom…she says rivers wash away sin. I don't know about that. Be nice, though." He turned to Aaron. "I didn't want to do it. You think that… sounds dumb. I know ya do. But it's the truth. I didn't want to. Even…when I was in the middle of doing it."

"Tell it to the judge, Casey."

"I'm not…gonna make it that far."

"Not the judge I'm talking about."

"Now you're righteous? One minute, you're sleeping with another man's girlfriend. Now you think you're…you're holier than thou."

Casey let out a brief laugh, then grimaced and brought both hands to his wound. "You did something wrong too. Ya don't get to hide from that. Now you owe me one." He pointed at the weak spot in the ice. "You're gonna help me over there. You're…gonna finish this."

The adrenalin Aaron felt earlier was long gone. There had been a flash of satisfaction—a few minutes worth, if that—at the end of the hunt. An ill reward for the effort. Anger had permeated the chase from the start, but waned after he saw how helpless his target had become. Now he felt nothing short of horror; a grave weight tearing loose the bindings of his sinking heart. He understood Casey's intention, and asked himself, *Is this murder? Is it suicide, or an accident? God, what is this? What IS this?*

Casey reached out for a hand. Aaron cautiously offered one and helped him sit. As Casey rose, he clenched a hand to his abdomen and, for an instant, his face became a true visage of pain. Then his muscles slackened, and eyes began to lose focus.

Aaron's hope and fear momentarily locked in contest, wanting it to be over, but afraid of seeing the end.

"Get me…over there." Casey managed to say.

"Yeah, I—"

"Hurry."

Aaron complied. First slinging Casey's arm around his shoulder, holding his wrist tight, then hoisting up his weight. Casey offered a handful of wobbly steps as the duo shuffled toward the tree. The ice cracked—a quick, dull echo—when they neared the weak spot where the hidden water spun and eddied too fast for anything but a thin freeze.

The two men stood together, one giving his strength to hold up the other.

Casey let go of the pressure on his abdomen. His hand fell, dripping by his side. He viewed the steaming flow from his belly one final time.

"My mom's gonna be sad. My dad…he won't care. But my mom's gonna be sad." Tears fell for a moment longer. Then Casey straightened himself as best he could and shrugged off Aaron's support, nearly collapsing as he did. A steadying breath. A couple of unsure steps—like a man well past inebriation—and Casey had maneuvered himself in front of Aaron, the weak ice now to his back. A glance over his shoulder verified his placement. He would fall into the space between the branches.

The men's eyes met. Casey's demeanor became distant and calm. So much so, Aaron questioned whether the man before him had led such a life as to make him consider death long ago.

"I…don't even know your name. You could at least…tell me."

"I'm Aaron." For a second, he felt he should reach out his hand. Another situation perhaps. Another life.

"Aaron, you know the thing my mom said about rivers? Do you think that's from the Bible, or did she make it up?"

"I…I don't remember reading that. Maybe I'll look it up someday."

Casey nodded weakly, almost imperceptibly. White lines popped into existence on the ice behind him. Aaron took a step back.

"I hope it's true."

"Yeah, I do—"

"Cuz I've got one sin left." Casey's hands flashed out and hooked into Aaron's coat. He jerked, once and hard, and brought Aaron against him as he toppled backward. Aaron stammered an excited "H-hey, *hey!*" as he grabbed for the nearest branch and felt his fingertips graze against smooth wood.

The two hit the ice as one. The weak spot shattered like glass and the river greedily lapped at them with wide, wet arms and pulled them down.

The cold hit first. Icy water soaked through Aaron's clothes and flooded his boots until every inch of his skin was bathed in a frigid rush. Immediately, the current took hold of them. Aaron bobbed once to the surface, only to have the broken edge of the hole strike the back of his skull. Then he was under, and the river whisked both men downstream.

The cold cut into Aaron's eyes as he watched a shifting ray of light move beyond reach. A voice screamed in his mind: *Don't lose sight of the hole!* The next second, his feet struck a massive stone and he spun away from the light. He turned one-hundred and eighty degrees, where an unseen finger of wood stabbed the right side of his neck. A cry of pain cost him half the air in his lungs.

He grasped the branch that injured him—too thin, he felt it crack and begin to give—then shot forth his other hand and managed to take hold further up where the branch was the thickness of his wrist.

Now anchored, Aaron's body whipped around again, and he felt a massive jerk that almost pulled loose his grip. There was more than the river working against him. His enemy still had a hold.

Casey had one hand clamped to Aaron's coat, the other fumbled at his body, searching for the tether which bound them against the current.

Aaron still had a grip on the thin branch that struck his neck and the larger limb which held his place. He twisted the smaller off completely and turned it into a weapon, thrusting at the hand which held fast to his coat. He struck again and again, but the water slowed the attack and sullied his aim. After a half-dozen attempts, it was clear the hand would not budge. He cocked back his arm and took one reckless swing at the dark shape of Casey's head. His strike found its target. The blunted wood grazed down the side of Casey's skull and added a bit of blood to the water but did nothing to dislodge him.

Worse, the force of Aaron's strike jarred his grip on the more solid branch, and the slick wood began to slide through his hand. He let go of his weapon—the current sent it careening off into the dark—and managed to get both hands locked back onto the limb. He pulled, trying to move himself up the branch to the opening in the ice, but the river pulled harder.

Desperation, a thing Aaron had never truly known, strangled him like a noose. His lungs seemed to stretch and tear, eager to expel the increasingly useless air inside them. The hands of his rival clawed their way up his body. The muted glow of a storm-struck day filtered through the ice above him, dangling a promise of life just out of reach.

The elements of the situation amassed, and a desolate quieting seemed to signal the approach of Death. Not yet tangible, but soon. The Reaper had begun to materialize, eager to claim the one whose final seconds ticked away.

Bubbles escaped Aaron's nose as the last of his breath fled. Casey's hand hooked over his shoulder. In the flickering shadows beneath the ice, the face of his nemesis rose before him.

Fleshless bone. Empty eyes. A grinning, ancient skull that could only belong to the Grim Reaper of Souls. Corporeal now. As real as the icy waters that flowed around him.

Aaron squeezed his eyes shut against the wavering sight of Death, but he heard him all the same. "I'm here. Here! And I'll not leave alone!"

Aaron's lungs were sucked tight and begging for breath. His mind, a wildly spinning panic. Still, the voice crashed into him: "I go with my prize! Look, Aaron. Look!" No choice then. He hung by two fingers to the frayed end of his rope. Damn the fear. If this truly was the end, if bearing witness to Death's face was the price to enter Heaven, he would endure it. Aaron opened his eyes and saw salvation.

Casey was there. The shadows couldn't conceal the madness that had surfaced at the end. The rush of water couldn't mute the sound of his scream. Out it came; hatred, fueled by the wrong done to him in his life, reflected inward by the wrong he'd done to others, finally cast out of his soul like poison milked from a wound. With the cry came life-giving breath.

Unlike Aaron, who'd lost half his air in the first seconds of submersion, Casey had retained a complete, albeit nearly depleted, lungful. In an instinctive moment of preservation, Aaron redoubled his grip on the anchor-branch with his right hand and, with his left, grasped the back of Casey's neck and pulled his head forward. He locked his mouth onto that of his opponent and his aching lungs swelled with air.

A second was all it took to complete the mouth-to-mouth. Aaron let go of Casey. His enraged expression had turned to utter disbelief. He sucked in a breath, but there was no breath to be had. His hands shot to his mouth. Too late to protect it from the drowning invasion which came to his lungs. No longer anchored, the river took hold of him and, head thrashing and arms in a frenzy, Casey slid away into the black.

Aaron wasted no time. His stolen breath offered seconds only. His numb fingers scarcely registered the feel of the branch as he began to climb sideways back toward the hole.

For the first time, he realized the mouths of his boots were flayed open and acting like a sail in the moving water. He kicked, a single time with each leg, and the river obliged to relieve him of the encumbrance.

Light increased as he moved toward the opening. More branches offered handholds. When Aaron came to the break, he reached up and slapped his forearm onto the ice. The thin ice gave out and the river yanked him backward. He caught the edge again—this time with his hand instead of the bend of his arm—and the jagged ice cut into his palm like broken glass.

He pulled again and the ice held. Brought both hands to the fractured edge and did a final chin-up to bring his face even with the hole. One arm out, hooked at the elbow. The second arm out, and he fought the defying current for a final time when his face breached the surface, and he drew in a yawning gasp.

Within a minute he'd struggled his way onto the ice, crawled to a safe distance from the break, and collapsed.

His body begged for a moment of peace. A well-deserved rest after the drowning struggle. No respite, however. Not yet. The cold struck again, just as it had when he'd plunged into the river. Now the chill of his soaked clothes held the winter freeze tight to his body. Worse, the wind had shifted. The calm in the ravine had been swept out by the storm and the frigid air whipped by, stealing what little of his heat remained.

Aaron sat, brought up his knees and made himself small against the cold. One spot of comparative warmth announced itself. A trickle ran down the right side of his neck. The cold had numbed the wound and contracted the vessel. Still the blood came. He pressed his palm against the source and wondered how much he'd given to the river.

He eyed the opening. The blowing snow was quickly filling the hole with slush. Soon there would be nothing but a scar on the ice. Then it would drift over. Come Spring, it would melt and disappear, as if nothing had happened here. However, Spring would reveal as well as conceal. It would be the season to discover Casey's body.

He's dead by now. He's not him. He's…a corpse.

The thought was massive. It filled the sky. Crushed the horizon. And it wouldn't stop.

Heather's dead, too. She's dead. Casey's dead. I should be dead.

Aaron questioned how long he'd been under. Minutes only. Two? No, it seemed like hours. A lifetime. To survive such a thing was a gift. But to sit on the ice and freeze into a mound would be an insult against the one who offered it.

He shoved aside thoughts of death. The event wasn't real yet. This was the stun. The initial sting of a slap, not the pain which followed. *Get out of here,* he thought, then spoke aloud "Get out."

Ahead of him lay the wall of the ravine. The path he'd taken down could be used for ascent, but it would take time, and a strength he was no longer certain he possessed. And upon reaching the summit? His truck was in the ditch. Aaron felt for his keys and found them still secured to a belt loop by a mountaineering clip. Maybe the truck would start. He'd crank the heat and wait for a car to pass. Maybe it wouldn't, and the next passerby would find his rigid body.

All the maybes would be answered in time. But first things first. Stand up.

Aaron moved on his hands and knees to the trunk of the fallen tree and used it to pull himself to his feet. He made his way toward the drift—the half-beaten path which still rose to the level of his ribs—walking on legs that felt like they'd fallen asleep from the knees down. *No way*, his mind told him *This isn't even the hard part. No w—*

He shook his head and killed the thought. Slapped his hands together and rubbed some heat into them. Then he began kicking his way through the bank with numb, stockinged feet.

As Aaron beat his way through the powder, his mind returned to what he'd seen in the river. The embodiment of Death. Little use in denying the sight. Those arguments would come later, if there were a later. For now, the memories were clear. The dead, penetrating stare of The Reaper's skull. His voice, heavy and deep, like the knell of church bells echoing up from a stone well. Yes, he'd seen Death and Death had seen him. Yet here he was, tortured body and all, still alive.

There had to be meaning to it. More than simply surviving his foe to meet his own end minutes later. There was purpose at work. To suffer is to appreciate, he had once heard as a youth in Sunday school. And, oh man, after this test he would define appreciation: for every breath he could blow out as casually as he took in; every twiddle of the toes, bare in the warm air of his apartment; the solidity of the very ground he stood on. The appreciation would go on and on if—*God please*—he was allowed to go on.

At that thought, his legs gave out.

He'd attempted a step forward and may as well been placing weight on a peg leg. There was no report from his foot. No confirmation if it had even moved. His hands went out to brace but had nothing to push against and simply stabbed into the snow to a shoulder's depth.

Aaron sank into the soft white bank and the sides of the path collapsed behind him. He came to a halt with his chin resting on the snow, head craned back far enough so he was facing the top of the ravine.

If someone were to look down over the edge at that very moment, they would see what appeared to be a mask made of flesh, peeking up from the drift. If that same someone—say a local farmer who'd seen the vehicles and followed the footprints, or an officer who'd been searching the outskirts of town after a crime—looked over the edge five minutes later, they would see nothing but a shallow groove, already filling in with falling and blowing snow.

Aaron pushed against the drift, and managed to elevate his body a few inches, only to sink back down without the support of his useless legs. A nightmare thought swept through his mind; *I'll never stand up again.*

He tried to will his legs into action, but they were gone. He threw himself into a futile battle against the snow, burning through the little energy he had left in a frantic series of movements aimed at nothing but a vague defiance of his situation.

At the point of exhaustion, he closed his eyes while drawing in deep, cold breaths. A moment's worth of rest was all he wanted. Fatigue began to envelope him in a welcoming, soft darkness. The tiny warmth on his neck became an interesting counterpoint to the shell of freezing clothes covering the rest of his body. Even the overwhelming cold had begun to change; not the clench of Winter's hard hand, but an anesthetic embrace to rid him of care and pain. The sound of the wind began to fade.

Not yet. I want to breathe some more. Just a little more.

In a diminished voice, he called out "Help…help." Eyelids fluttered. Slowly lifted halfway. He viewed the top of the ravine. Empty.

Beyond it, naked trees shook in the wind. Above the trees, a towering gray sky.

His gaze fell to the path before him. Such a short, impossible distance. The base of the wall at its terminus may as well have been the foothills of a mountain.

As he breathed a little more, then a little more, a shadow slid down the wall of the ravine. Aaron blinked, squinted at it. It was there, a darker gray in the dull colors of the storm. He followed the shadow up the embankment and paused right before he came to its source. Death would be perched there, grinning down, ragged cloak fluttering in the wind. He was sure of it. All a trick. No purpose after all, and no point in viewing this terror again. Once had been enough.

Aaron closed his eyes. The snow blew across his face and into his mouth, where it melted in the lingering warmth. Tiny puffs of air were lost in the wind as it screamed through the river's trough.

He hadn't seen further shadows join the first, but they had. He couldn't view the brilliant colors on the victor's side of the climb he was unable to make. Yet they shone all the same, flashing through the gloom in glorious defiance of a darkening day.

--Alex Vayle is a Fargo author who enjoys writing haunting, character-driven tales of supernatural suspense. His influences range from Hemingway to Stephen King, yet each story is uniquely Vayle. When not writing, he enjoys nature, time with his wife and four children, and caring for patients at a local hospital. His debut collection, *Among the Stray*, can be purchased online wherever books are sold. Find him on Twitter @alexandervayle or shoot an email to alexandervayle@gmail.com

The Christmas Phantom

By Barbara Bustamante

When I turned six, nothing was the same. Daddy lost his job at the school. Mommy told me that two schools became one and they only needed one office. Daddy wanted to move to the mountains where he grew up. Mommy worked in the school kitchen and said she could get a job anywhere. I hated leaving our house and all my friends to travel across the country in a camper that we had to set up every night. I missed my bedroom and all my toys and games. I couldn't even take my bike along. Most of all I missed my friends at school. We were friends FOREVER!

So we had a big sale and sold everything that didn't fit in our van. I said goodbye to all my friends, then early in the morning we left for the mountains. It was a long ride that took two days. We arrived at a big campground and, at first, living in the camper was kind of fun. Something like playing house in the woods at Grandma's. The bus picked me up every morning and the kids at school were nice to me. But after a while I was homesick for all the things I used to do on Halloween and Thanksgiving. I had little hope for Christmas.

Snow and cold greeted us one morning, but most of it melted by the time I got home from school. The owners of the campground felt sorry for us since we were the only ones left in the campground. They had a cabin on wheels that we could live in, which was a lot warmer and Mommy didn't have to carry water every day. I also had a real bed to sleep in.

One day after I got off the bus, I found a box by the front door. I told Mommy and when we opened it, we found a tiny Christmas tree inside. There was no note - just the tree. I was happy to have a little tree to decorate. When Daddy got home from job hunting, we set it on the coffee table in the living room. It was so pretty all by itself. It reminded me of the big Christmas trees in Minnesota.

A couple days later there was another box by the door. This one had a small string of colored lights. We moved the tree to a small table by the wall so we could plug in the lights. The box also contained some glass bulbs, a rope of silver garland, and a small golden star that fit on the top of the tree. After we decorated the tree, I spent a long time gazing at the tree and its beauty as it sparkled and filled the dark room with light. Oh, how I missed our big tree back home. Then Mom had to remind me to finish my homework and get to bed on time.

Christmas was over a week away, but another box was by the door on Friday. It contained a box of Christmas cards and a book of stamps. That night Mommy and I wrote notes and addressed the cards to Grandma and Grandpa, Aunt Janice, Uncle Warren, and Aunt Sandy. We also sent one to our old neighbor Marcy. Nor could I forget my friends Twila and Christy, my teacher Mrs. Johnson from back home, and Mom's old boss Mrs. Green who made the best chocolate chip cookies. I got to take the stack of cards to the mailbox in the morning.

I wondered if there would be another box by the door on Monday. And there was. This one had a big paper plate with Christmas cookies and packets of hot cocoa and spiced cider. The cookies were in shapes of stars, trees, Santa Claus, and bells covered with frosting and brightly colored sprinkles. They smelled so good that you just wanted to gobble them up. They tasted so good. It would have been fun to decorate them with Mommy.

A couple days later, everyone at school was excited about Christmas coming. For a long time, everything was new to me. I just wanted something like it used to be. The boxes at the door were fun, but somehow, I wanted more. The box at the door that day had a bright red plastic tablecloth with napkins, mistletoe, window clings, a scented candle, Christmas kitchen towels and potholders, and a festive centerpiece for the table on Christmas Day. Mommy and I laughed a lot while decorating the cabin. With still days away, it started to look like Christmas.

I had no school the day before Christmas. I helped Mommy clean and wash dishes then I took a short walk around the campground. It was cold, but most of the snow had melted. After lunch there was a knock at the door. It seemed odd because there was hardly anyone in the campground. Mommy and I went to the door and all we saw was a pair of legs flying over the deck railing. A big box had been left by the door. Inside we found a large ham, a bag of potatoes, a jar of gravy, a can of vegetables, a bag of frozen rolls, and a frozen pumpkin pie. At the bottom of the box was a card that said:

> *Hope Your Holiday Is Simply Glowing*
>
> *Thank you to the Morris Family for allowing us to partake in the true spirit of this joyous season. We have truly enjoyed bringing you a little happiness during troubled times.... with special joy that just keeps growing!*

Happy Holidays

Love from:

The Christmas Phantom and Company

-- Barbara Bustamante holds a BUS Degree in Food and Nutrition from North Dakota State University. She is semi-retired and lives in Moorhead, MN with her cat.

The Day I had A Hot Date And We Fell Out Of The Sky

By Wayne McFarland

A hot date and two cases of beer was all it had taken to get us into this mess. That and the completely unauthorized use of a military snowplow.

When the roads were clear, it was a 5-hour winter's drive from my airbase in North Dakota to Minneapolis where a lady friend had taken up residence. After a rather breathy invitation, a New Year's Eve party in Minneapolis beckoned. Actually, it did more than beckon...it shouted with the irresistible siren call that only the young and on the hunt can truly hear. Problem was that while New Year's Eve Day dawned clear, the night before a blizzard had come through, depositing feet of snow. Roads were closed in all directions.

I was in the Air National Guard at the time, stationed at an airport in mid-North Dakota. The airport was part civilian, part military. It was blazingly hot in the summer. This was balanced by it being cold as hell in the winter, with armpit deep snow. More often than not, this snow was deposited by ferocious blizzards which would build huge drifts and effectively drop temperatures to 30 below zero.

The airport's runways were snow-blocked as well as the roads that morning, but I went up to the tower anyway. At that time, hitch-hiking was not considered a sure way to meet a serial killer. Better yet, some wag had come up with the successful idea of occasionally scoring a hitch on a private plane. That's of course if you didn't mind hanging out at an airport until you found an amenable pilot and didn't care where, exactly, you landed.

I figured it was worth a shot. To my surprise, when I walked in to the tower's connected "ready room," there were two guys looking at a flight plan log and arguing about flying to Minneapolis.

One of them, the older one, had a broken-veined, red face and a sparse comb over. The younger guy was being a real dick, whining about getting to Minneapolis for New Year's Eve and clearly implying that it was the other one's fault they were stuck.

The older guy was beyond exasperated. "The runways are blocked with snow; what the hell do you expect me to do?"

Ah. I walked up to them and allowed as how I might be able to solve that problem, my price being to hitch a ride on their flight to Minneapolis. They blinked at me. "Sure," said the comb over guy.

I called my buddy Sargent Johnson, who was initially skeptical due to a couple of schemes gone badly awry in the past. He was in charge of a lot of the base's military vehicles including snowplows. I explained my plan. "No!" he responded instantly. "Goddamn it, no! That's unauthorized use of military equipment and I won't do it! Besides, what's in it for me?"

Short negotiations resulted in a two cases of beer commitment on my side. Ten minutes later my new traveling companions and I were treated to the sight of a huge snowplow, military off-green, clearing the small craft runway we needed to use. The blizzard had not hit Minneapolis, so once airborne we were good in the sense that we could land upon arrival.

My new companions were astonished, delighted. Their 6-seater Cessna was tied down outside a hangar and had, apparently, weathered the storm quite well. "Give us 5 minutes. Then come on out and hop aboard."

Hop aboard I did. Mr. Comb-Over fired up the engine and we took off, they whooping with delight and me congratulating myself for being so damn tricky.

A few minutes later, I wasn't feeling quite so damn tricky.

"Just fly the plane! Dad, PLEASE! PLEASE! JUST FLY THE FUCKING PLANE!"

The older guy was shouting incoherently and beating on the plane's dashboard. The younger guy, riding shotgun in the Cessna was, it seemed, his son.

Sitting in back I kept thinking how quiet things were between the shouts. Not surprising, since our only engine had shut down. We had been flying along smugly harmonizing off-color verses to "Row, Row, Row Your Boat." Then in an instant we became a winged rock.

"There, there!" shouted the son pointing, "on the left, on the left, there's a flat field!" Since our landing gear was fixed like a 3-wheeled tricycle, if the selected snow-covered field wasn't flat as a board we were well and truly screwed. A belly landing was not an option. We couldn't see any roads, which might have provided salvation. This being the case, I decided that right then was probably not the time to mention snow usually covered deep furrows on many of the fields, the furrows having been humped up by farmers harvesting the last of the sugar beet crop.

A Mayday was called. And called again. It was pretty clear we were going in.

"Son, I'm so sorry. I'm so sorry. I'm sorry." The son did not respond. He now sat silently; fixedly staring out the side window as we went down. Our weeping pilot started cursing, screaming, mashing the key in the starter again and again only to hear the engine grind.

I swear to God we were just a few feet off the deck when the engine emitted a loud chuff and a bang! and fired right up. We flew back to our starting point. The engine would stutter occasionally. "C'mon, you bitch, c'mon, c'mon!" the pilot kept muttering. His hands were trembling on the yoke. When the airport came in sight, the son reached out and covered his dad's shaking hands with his own.

We landed without further incident.

"That stupid asshole should be dead." I was standing next to the plane. It was now hangared and being looked over by a mechanic, who had just rendered his opinion of the pilot. We both gazed through the window at Mr. Comb Over's car weaving uncertainly out of the airport.

"Well, I'm glad he's not." I responded, deeply sincere. "Why do you say that?"

"I was watching when he was getting ready to leave." The mechanic shook his head. "The dumb shit didn't pre-flight check his plane. He just had a couple of other idiots jump in and they took off."

"So?" I responded. Not being a pilot myself, I added "It must have been 20 below outside; can hardly blame the guy."

The mechanic glared over, clearly moving me from his "O.K. Guy" into his "Idiot" mental column.

"His fucking plane sat out in a blizzard all night. I guarantee you the engine compartment got packed with show. The engine got hot; the snow melted and screwed up the engine's electrical. What a dipshit. He's lucky he's not scattered all over the ground…along with his two buddies."

"Yes," I agreed. "Lucky indeed."

When I got back to the airport a bit later after a sojourn to purchase the two cases of payment beer, I found that the clearing of the small craft runway had opened an opportunity for a number of other small craft pilots who also wanted to get to Minneapolis that day.

All the newly gathered pilots were buzzing about the highly unusual Mayday call; shaking their heads over what did indeed turn out to be the reason for it. When I announced I had been on the plane but not the pilot, I got multiple offers for a ride-along to Minneapolis. A few hours later I found myself at the party. And there, looking beautiful, as I recall, was my lady friend.

She took my hands. "I'm so glad you came. I didn't think you'd be able to make it, what with the blizzard. Did you have any trouble getting here?"

"Not a bit," I responded.

-- Wayne McFarland wandered away from a small, mid-western town some years ago. With no planning at all, his history is one of stumbling into one bog after another from the Dakotas to California, from Pamplona to Paris. His main claim to fame is mostly and surprisingly not being dead, plus getting involved with a lot of strange stuff, usually unwillingly or by accident.

A Walk on All Hallows' Eve
by Jason Bursack

The Gaelic word Samhain *means 'summer's end' and refers to a festival originating in Celtic lands that spread throughout Northwestern Europe – including Brittany.*

It was my love for historic buildings that led me to attend the funeral of a man I didn't know. I stood outside the old church in a cool, autumn breeze, breathing deeply, enjoying the crisp scent of dead leaves on the soft wind, the tinge of wood smoke in the air. An Episcopal church, St. George's, built in this quaint Midwestern town in the late 1800s. Why the town – I was here on business, had an afternoon and evening to kill, and what a way to spend Halloween.

The church, built of gray brick, had a single spire, vaulted roof, and of course stained-glass windows. It was difficult to take them in from the outside, as it generally is with stained glass. The church's website had indicated the original windows had been replaced with windows recovered from European churches bombed during the world wars, and yet somehow remained intact. This of course increased my desire to enter the building, but there was some kind of event going on, formal, perhaps a wedding, and I was in back staying out of everyone's way.

I first heard her voice as I stood so close to one of the lower windows that my nose might have touched it had I leaned forward. All she said was, "Hey, mister?"

I turned and saw a short, young woman, maybe twenty-two. Her hair, wavy and dyed stark black, came down just past her shoulders. She was a bit scrawny, wore dark eyeliner and mascara but no other makeup that I could see, ratty jeans and a black, zipped sweatshirt, and into its front pockets she had thrust her hands, thin wrists protruding a pale inch before her arms were covered by the sleeves of her sweatshirt. Her dark eyes were a little wide-set and contained perhaps a hint of latent terror. She rose up and down on the balls of her feet, her canvas sneakers crunching against a layer of red, yellow, and brown leaves. The breeze picked up, encircling her ankles with a small vortex of autumnal detritus.

"Yes?" I asked. I decided she was pretty.

"Did you know him?"

"Who?"

"Good. You mind coming to a funeral? See, I don't want to talk to anyone who knew him and, if you're with me, I can just pretend I'm too sad to answer questions."

Her voice was deadpan, as though she spent effort to minimize the musical quality of the human voice. I simply frowned at her.

Her eyes flashed downward only for a second. "Sorry, I know it's kind of a weird question."

I shrugged. "It's fine."

"I'd really appreciate it if you'd join me. It'll be a short funeral, I promise."

Her dark eyes spoke of something, a kind of longing, perhaps. I don't know if it was the sheer boredom of being trapped in this town for a day, if I felt pity on her, or if both of these urges were enhanced by my desire to see the inside of the church, but for some reason I agreed. To go to a funeral.

"All right."

"Great." She took my arm and lowered her head, mumbled at our shoes. "We'll just go in like this. I'm going to sniffle to ward them off. Just to warn you, though, I might actually start crying for real."

"It's fine," I said again, walking with her to the front of the church along a concrete path.

I was not dressed for a funeral. But, then again, neither was she, and we were together now, so it would have been more awkward had I been in a jacket and tie like many of the men in attendance. We went in the front door, through a small crowd that mingled with hushed voices full of reverence in that way of funeral attendees, received a card from a greeter.

The sanctuary was about half full, an open casket in front.

"I want to go up," she whispered. My funeral date and I walked up the center aisle.

It was only now that I began to fully absorb the absurdity of my situation. I'd been to plenty of funerals, of course. Grandparents, the parents of good friends, at this point in my life even several friends my own age, lives lost to tragic accidents, early disease, or to their own misery. You get enough of them under your belt and it becomes easy to walk up and be somber.

The deceased, Samuel Rourke according to the card, had died at twenty-eight. He had a doughy build, had begun to prematurely bald, and there was a kind of cheer visible in his face that persisted even beyond the mortician's attempt at the creation of postmortem peace.

The girl on my arm erupted in sobbing. She clutched me, convulsed, her pain and grief so raw that my own eyes moistened by proxy. I put my arm around her shoulders and let her collapse into me as she cried. After perhaps two minutes she fully recovered with the same suddenness with which she had burst into tears. "Let's go sit down," she whispered, dabbing her eyes and face with the provided tissue. We did.

She was right – it was a short funeral. Less than an hour. A man in a suit came up front, told us why we were there, and then there was a song. A blonde girl and boy, late teens or early twenties, played a hymn, her on violin and he on piano, surprisingly lovely for an amateur endeavor. Friends and relatives offered short speeches. They spoke of the deceased's gregariousness, his cleverness, his way of always helping anyone he could. By the end of the ceremony, I felt he must have been a very kind person. My funeral date sat quietly next to me, looking down at her hands in her lap, sniffing occasionally. When the service was done, she whispered to me, "We need to leave as quickly as possible, okay?"

I nodded and after the procession had completed, we made our way out. We were stopped only by one determined couple, right before the exit. "And how did you know Sam?"

I took answering the question to be my responsibility, particularly since the girl was still staring at her shoes. "I worked with him once. Such a great guy. Clever as heck." I thought about adding, 'tragic, what happened,' but I of course had no idea what had happened, so this could have had the potential to horribly misfire.

"He sure was," said the man, a look of reminiscence on his face.

The girl on my arm shuddered into a sob, drawing looks of sudden sympathy.

"If you'll excuse us," I said.

"Of course, of course."

Clear of the church, she looked up at me. "I'm fine. That one was fake," she said, though her eyes were still moist.

I nodded at her, unsure what to say next.

"We can walk to the cemetery. That should be good timing, get us there after he's buried. It's a ways away. I want to see the grave, but I don't want to disturb the family, of course." She then began to walk, and as she still held my arm, and I did not resist, I went with her. It occurred to me there were worse ways I could kill an evening in a bland town than on a walk with a pretty girl, even if one wracked by grief.

The sun began to set the lightly clouded horizon ablaze. The air's chill increased and I pulled the zipper of my light jacket to mid-chest. We walked. "My name is Will," I said.

"Sam."

"Just like the deceased. How did you know him? Or, do you want to talk about something else?"

"I didn't actually know him."

I gave a light, involuntary cough. "Ah, forgive me for assuming."

"No, no, it's fine," she said, her voice relaxed for the first time. "That totally makes sense you'd think that. But really what is going on is I was a subscriber to his YouTube channel."

I turned to her for a moment as we walked. She was just the right height that the very top of her head was immediately under my nose and I smelled the remnants of a floral shampoo, lilac, or violet, mixed in with the natural, pleasantly bitter scent of her hair. Auburn roots were just beginning to show at the part in the middle of her head. A pity, honestly, that she dyed it so black. She didn't look up, which perhaps was good. I wasn't sure what kind of expression I had on my face.

"I know it seems weird," she said. "But his videos were really meaningful to me."

"How so?"

"And can you imagine me having to say that at the funeral? Yes, mother of the deceased, I traveled six hundred miles by train to your son's funeral because I liked his videos. So, that's why I wanted you to come with me."

"Mm."

"And, you totally seemed like you didn't know him very well, standing there studying that church window."

"An understatement."

She laughed, sniffled, adorable, wiped her nose with the sleeve of her sweatshirt, her hands scrunched up inside the elastic wrists, thumbs poked out through holes she had cut or punched. "Anyway, Sam – and I mean him Sam, not me Sam – was trying, I guess, basically, to discover the meaning of life on his YouTube channel. He did these long, rambling videos where he'd talk about comparative religion, human history, anthropology, even poetry. Like he was on this desperate search for some kind of code that would reveal the true meaning of life." She looked up at me, her dark eyes piercing, breathtakingly haunted. "He kept asking the question – what story do you live in?"

I did not have words, feeling lost in her eyes. Her eyes had me good in my chest.

She looked away and I recovered. "That's an interesting question."

"Right, and so the idea was, he was unraveling this hidden code that's stitched into the warp and weft of the universe. The human aspect of the universe, anyway. And he only had one more video left. He said he'd finally figured it out. Added it all up, put together the final truth. Out of all the possible stories, the one true story. But then…" Her voice cracked.

I gently continued the sentence for her. "He passed away."

"He tripped on a shoe and fell down a flight of stairs, broke his neck and died on the spot."

The flatness in her voice astonished me. "That's terrible."

She stared at the ground, scuffing at the pavement with her sneakers as we walked. "You know what's dumb even is that it was his own shoe."

"Okay."

"I just…I don't know. For some reason I just find that extra awful in this weird poetic sense."

"I can see that, I guess."

We walked in silence for a while along what looked like the main artery through town, a light breeze whisking leaves around us, the smell of fires intensifying. The funeral procession began to pass us on the street, the black hearse followed up by a train of many cars. Sam put her head down when they went by and I felt compelled to put my arm around her shoulders as we walked, as though it would somehow shelter her from the stark reality of this grim parade. We didn't speak for perhaps twenty minutes.

"Take a left here," she finally said, sliding out from under my arm. We turned, side by side now, onto a street lined by houses that looked thirty or forty years old. I found the neighborhood beautiful. It reminded me of my own far-gone youth, a sunny time well before I began my long series of poor decisions. The sun lowered, the sky dimmed, and streetlamps began to flicker on.

"I was at an awful time in my life when I discovered Sam," she said. She scratched her chin with the thumbnail of her right hand and then bit at the cuff of the sleeve of her sweatshirt for a moment. She did not need to tell me that she had attempted suicide, or at least thought seriously about it. "He helped me. A lot."

"That's great you found him."

She stared at the ground. "I never even left a comment on his videos. I wish I had."

I wondered if I should put my arm around her again but the space she had put between us suggested otherwise, so we just kept walking in the twilight. The porch lights of houses began to come on. In the near distance, a man wearing a comically ill-fitted gray robe walked toward us, a small child in a white sheet scampering at his side. A neighborhood like this, I figured, would have the trick-or-treaters out in droves.

"I'm glad you got to come to his funeral," I said.

"Me too, yeah."

The man approached with his child. His ball cap contrasted the cheap robe that went to his knees, revealing his faded blue jeans. Face ruddy, full of cheer. He gave us a hearty wave before bolstering himself with an affected look of alarm. "Be warned, strangers!" he called with vigor. "The risen souls of the dead return on All Hallows' Eve to visit their homes!" He grinned and pointed at his kid. A girl of maybe five or six, brilliant brown curls, missing front tooth, smiled gleefully. The sheet she wore had holes cut for her head and arms, went down to her ankles, revealing pink boots fringed with white fuzz. The girl giggled with glee. The man kept pointing downward, whispered loudly, "Soul of the dead, right here."

I grinned. "Fearsome."

Sam smiled wryly in a way I found marvelously attractive. "I tremble in terror, sir."

We all laughed, and they passed us. Sam and I continued our walk.

The twilight dimmed, and soon the only light in the sky was a fading glow in the far west. Light clouds wafted in, and the moon rose behind them. Halloween characters of a wide range of ages came out in droves, children dressed as superheroes and monsters, classic and new. Vampires, neon-suited warriors, anthropomorphic oddities, Frankenstein's creation. My award for best costume – a father and mother as Pac-Man and Ms., their five children three dots and two ghosts. Sam and I took them all in with muted joy, making small comments, this one or that one is neat, this one or that one silly, some of them making us laugh together. I brushed my hand against hers and she did not startle, but out of respect for her youth and her grief I did not take it. She also did not take mine and clasp.

We had walked for probably two hours when our road took a hard right into a forested area. Before us was a lamplit steel gate, one of its doors open enough for a person to slink sideways through. We had reached the cemetery.

"The gate is unlocked, but is the cemetery open?" I asked.

She took my hand, shaking her head. "Come on."

We slipped through the gate and she pulled me down a trail. The light of the moon through the thin clouds showed me the rows of headstones. "Stop," she said, at some point. I did.

She let go of my hand, took her cell phone from the rear pocket of her jeans, flicked on the diode, and walked among the headstones, eventually finding a grave. Knelt down in front of it and wept softly.

I turned, walked a ways to give her space. Went to a headstone across the path and glanced down to see if I could read the name, but it was too dark, and I did not want to disturb her with my own light. I just stood in the chilling air, taking in the place. In all appropriateness, I heard a single hoot of an owl. After about ten minutes she returned to my side. "Okay, one more thing," she said. The rising moon was becoming brighter and I could see her eyes glimmer.

"What's that?"

Standing here in this moonlit cemetery, she handed me, of all things, her cell phone. Her voice was even and calm. "We need to do his last video for him. I'll try my best to put the theory together."

* * *

Sam appeared blurry in the video, almost pixelated. Her pale face lit by the clouded moon was this device's only logical point of focus. She sat on the base of a statue near the cemetery's mausoleum, knees tucked to her chest, arms draped around her legs. A digital ghost.

She glanced to her right as though speaking to no one in particular. As though I was not there. "And is love really the center of the universe, the reason for all existence? The only thing we really need? I suppose I could hum a few lines from a Beatles song but…" She bowed her head, ran a hand through her hair before resting it wanly on her knee and looking off into the dark forest. "I don't really feel like it. I'm more of a Stones girl, anyway."

The owl hooted again and I knew she would find this appropriate, but I doubted the phone's microphone would have caught it.

"I like how you always said that science as an explanation was silly. That saying the Big Bang created the universe is kind of like saying that the morning creates the day. That science is a tool but it's become some kind of weird fetish, a new half-religion, a ginned-up excuse to call someone an idiot for having different opinions than you. And I was with you when you made your correction. I thought you were wrong when you said we don't need science at all to discern ultimate meaning but then, when you changed your mind, we Sams were in agreement."

She turned her head to her left now as though addressing a different portion of an audience. The audience that wasn't there. Or, I wondered, blinking – was she speaking to the myriad dead?

"But this really shouldn't be about me, should it. You died tragically before you could knit your theory together. I thought a moment ago I could do it for you, that I could synthesize everything you'd produced in my memory and make it make sense in the way you always made sense to me…" She sniffed and recovered. "And you brought me out of the depths of my darkness."

She paused, swallowed. I doubted that the phone would pick up the sundry sounds of night in a forest cemetery, the quiet cacophony of breeze and insects and rodents and the occasional nocturnal bird of prey.

"So, that isn't what this last video is about, then. I don't know the meaning of life any more than anyone else does now that you're dead. You were the only one who knew, and you took your secret to the grave."

A few tears escaped and, in the video, it looked like her eyes suddenly became larger and then blurred away completely for a second, the camera's autofocus struggling in the night.

"I think the thing I found most and also least interesting about you was your attempt at theodicy. For my newer viewers, that means, basically, an attempt to make evil make sense in a world where God is love. You tried, I don't know, maybe ten of them, but they always rang so hollow. I think you said once that it's possible that the best of all possible worlds could possibly be one in which evil and calamity exist, but I don't know if I'm saying that right. I'm not sure I care."

She wiped her tears with her sleeve, collected herself again with a deep breath. She looked up now, her eyes in the video becoming gleaming, featureless white points reflecting moonlight into the confused camera. "Here's what bothers me most. If God is love and that's the reason we exist, that everything exists, and I think that's where you were going, then of course why is there all this pain and death and misery? Why does a young, gorgeous soul like you go and trip on his own shoe and break his neck and die? And yes, I know that's everyone's problem, but here's my thing. If everything is meaningless, like we both thought once, then love is this sort of beautiful accident. It makes you stop and appreciate every act of love, and you stop wondering at all the evil and calamity because that's the default – that's just how things are. But if there is a higher power and that higher power is love and love is the ultimate, the destined union, the reason for everything, then all of a sudden the existence of calamity and evil have us asking why."

"Why?" she asked again, swallowing.

The forest made its sounds.

"I don't know," she said, looking right at the camera. "But I think embracing this unifying love might be better than the alternative. And I say this as someone who knows the alternative pretty well."

Sam hopped down from the statue and gave me a little nod. The video was complete. I took a couple steps toward her and handed her the phone.

"Thank you," she whispered.

"You're welcome," I said. Her eyes widened and her lips parted delicately. I'd not refuse the invitation. I pulled her to me and kissed her deeply, felt her body melt against mine, enjoyed her mouth and her muted sigh of submission. We parted and her face glowed with stark intensity, the ghost coming into true, haunting focus. She gasped and I think I did too, and we both looked up as the clouds revealed the full moon in all its vigor and intensity. I could not look away. I felt every crater of that faraway land imprinted on the bottom of my soul. I heard leaves rustle but still could not pull my mind free of the heavenly body.

When I could finally look down, she was gone.

* * *

The walk back was so cold my teeth chattered on and off. Amazing how as simple a thing as a kiss can make your knees feel weak hours later. I took deep breaths of cold air, clenched and unclenched my fingers, jogged a while, got my blood pumping. It's not that cold, I told myself. I'd just been outside a long time.

The trick-or treaters were mostly gone by now. There were some older kids still around, and half the houses had their lights turned off. Out of candy or went to bed.

I daydreamed about Sam, the purest fantasies a man of my age and experience could ever have, I supposed. I replayed in my mind our kiss, her eyes, her voice, the way she bared her soul *for me* first before putting it on YouTube, which was her stated intent. I did not once imagine undressing her and knew I never would.

A strange sight jolted me back to reality. I had reached the spot where I'd seen the gray-robed man and his daughter, must have been three hours ago, and I swore I saw the same kid ahead of me, that white sheet whirling like an angelic dust-devil. Not far from the kid, a woman broke into a quick walk to catch up. As I came closer I saw it was indeed the same child, perhaps with her mother now. I waved hello, and despite my shivering tried to appear as relaxed as I could as a strange man approaching a woman and child on a street at night.

She waved back, gave me a friendly, "Hey, nice night for a walk."

I smiled and we stopped under a streetlamp. I waved at the girl and she grinned at me. "Remember me?" I asked. She just laughed. I turned to the woman. "I saw her earlier tonight. With her dad?"

The woman laughed too. "Yes. She wanted to go back out again. It's her favorite holiday. I think she has more energy than both of us."

"I haven't given Halloween much thought in a long time."

"It's a funny story, really. Our church was going to ban it. Because pagans, or whatever."

I saw then the silver cross at her throat. Her hair looked ashy-blonde, the best I could tell in the orange streetlamp glow, up in Dutch braids that were starting to fall apart from the torments of the day. A turquoise headband covered the tops of her ears, her face elfin somehow, a beauty not stunning but might catch you off guard the second or third time you look.

"What happened?" I asked.

"Brittany would not have Halloween banned. I had to come up with a story. Called a meeting."

She had a clever smile on her face. I raised an eyebrow like go on.

"I told them about my Breton ancestors. The Vigil of All Saints, how they believed the souls of the dead were freed from purgatory for two days to visit their old homes. They attended the Black Vespers and then went in procession to the cemetery to pray and sing hymns for the dead. Late in the evening they set empty chairs around the table for their returning loved ones and recited the *De Profundis*. This was convincing enough, thought the ladies at church. So our Brittany has her Halloween, and of course it's the basis for her costume."

Brittany squealed and began to run in circles again, prompting both adults to laugh. I asked her mother, "I wonder what it would be like to feel that kind of simple joy again?"

She gave me a weary half-smile. "Who knows. I mean, we will someday, right? Jesus can come back and put the world to rights any day now, wipe away our tears and pain and all that." Her look then got bleak. "For those that want it, anyway."

I must have blinked or something because suddenly she softened, touched my arm. "I'm sorry. I just assume everyone around here is Christian. It's a tight neighborhood."

I just stood looking at her, flummoxed, fascinated by the notion that the inner peace that some of us, like Sam and me, never get, or maybe half-acquire after having scraped through a rough decade or two, is embraced by some people with no trouble at all.

But no. I was making assumptions. I had no knowledge of what had gone on in the depths of this woman's heart during the story of her life.

Brittany's sniffle and sigh broke the silence. Her mother scooped her up. "Well, I think it's time to go put you in the chair we have set for you at home. Or maybe just right to bed, huh?"

I still felt nearly mute but asked a silly question that could get them on their way again, a tactic to avoid an awkward and immediate clipping off of our encounter with a startling goodbye. "What's the *De Profundis*?"

Mother looked at daughter. "Shall we say it?"

They spoke together in practiced fashion, voices hauntingly musical.

* * *

Out of the depths have I cried unto thee, O Lord.

Lord, hear my voice: let thine ears be attentive to the voice of my supplications.

If thou, Lord, shouldest mark iniquities, O Lord, who shall stand?

But there is forgiveness with thee, that thou mayest be feared.

I wait for the Lord, my soul doth wait, and in his word do I hope.

My soul waiteth for the Lord more than they that watch for the morning: I say, more than they that watch for the morning.

***

And somehow I became one that watched for the morning, walking all night, jogging from time to time to stay warm. In the smallest hours, a light snow began to fall. I reached my hotel just as dawn broke on All Saints Day, packed my things, drank a couple cups of bleak hotel coffee, and called a rideshare to take me to the airport. I stood waiting on the white-dusted hotel lawn, frost and snow breaking beneath my shoes, the sun blazing gold in the distant east, and it may have been the lack of sleep or thinking about Sam still or what, but it was like the entirety of my life wound through my mind, from melancholy childhood to angry adolescence, an adulthood with ups and downs and joys and terrors, a rock bottom, my son who was eight now and I never saw, raised by a married couple who had moved to southern Oregon, of two coworkers who'd overdosed, of a car accident I'd survived but had killed three, of all of the times in life when we are scourged or blessed seemingly only by chance and are left stunned by the absurdity of reality, and could I do what Sam did and make that same choice, because her question was my question too, that enquiry that is the focus of so many of our dark nights – the existence of calamity and death have us asking why, why, why…

-- Jason Bursack is a writer living in Fargo, North Dakota. His work has also appeared in Embark Literary Journal.

A Paragon of Virtue

By William R. Bartlett

The quiet made me open my eyes. The last forecast I'd heard called for a brief, but heavy snowstorm and, judging by the lack of ambient noise, the weatherman had been spot on. Just like it did during my youth, this first snow of the season showed an uncanny ability to avoid Christmas, choosing instead to fall a couple days before New Year's Eve. I slipped out of bed, careful to keep from waking the lovely Al, and made my way downstairs.

Seamus eyed me from the breakfast table. "Good morning, Father."

"Morning, Seamus. Looks like snow." As usual, my droll humor sailed over his head, but I didn't mind. How else would I keep in practice? I strolled to the sliding glass door and studied the amount piled up on the patio table. "I'd say a good three inches. Maybe more."

He swallowed his last bit of peanut butter and jelly on toast. At least he'd had a hot breakfast.

I ambled to the front of our home and checked the parking area. Our townhome duplex didn't have a driveway, just an asphalt pad with enough room for two cars for us and a pair for our neighbors. Since we had only one vehicle and our neighbor hadn't arrived from her overnight job, most of the area lay under a pristine covering of the deceptive white stuff—pretty on top, but just waiting for the chance to turn into a frozen, treacherous layer below.

I turned back toward Seamus. "I want you to shovel the parking lot. Start with the porch and sidewalk, then do our neighbor's side. We need to be quick, so we can finish her side before she gets home. I'll join you after I've eaten."

"No, I'm busy. I have a game scheduled for today."

"If you do it soon and fast, you should have plenty of time. I'll feed the pets for you."

He sighed. "OK, Father."

Like everyone else almost out of high school, he's got an active, online social life. But push come to shove, he's still my son and he inherited my love of freshly fallen snow.

***

Seamus had been out long enough for me to finish my oatmeal and get dressed, making sure the coffee pot was filled and brewing, when he burst through the door, carrying a plastic, gallon-size ice cream container.

"Father, you've got to see what I found."

He opened the lid and my jaw dropped. "Where did you get this?"

"On the edge of our neighbor's parking. I'd just finished doing her side and I hit it when I lifted the shovel. Are we rich?"

I mentally thumbed through one of the binders of cash. If one of the bills said it was a hundred, all of them did. A chill grew in the pit of my stomach.

"Did you earn this money?"

"No."

"Then what makes you think it's ours?"

"Well… I found it."

"Listen to me very carefully." I grabbed both his shoulders and stared into his eyes. "You must never talk about this again, not to anyone, not at any time. Do you understand me?"

"But…"

I dug my fingers into his shoulders. "This is serious, Seamus. How do we know the people who left it there aren't criminals? And if they are, they won't hesitate to break in and kill us all, even the dog and cat, just to get that money. And they'll take your electronics, too. Got that?"

Seamus squirmed. "Father, you're hurting me."

"This is important." I loosened my grip. "Do you have any questions?"

"No."

"I swear, Seamus, I'll take a hammer and blowtorch to every one of your electronics if you don't obey. This could mean our lives, and I'm not joking." I took a deep breath. "Why don't you take the rest of the morning off and head back up to your room. I'll get what's left of the parking pad."

"But my game."

"We'll make a special exemption this time. Take your laptop to your room and play there. Got it?"

"OK, Father."

Seamus clomped up the stairs while I went to the door and looked out. No tire tracks on the street, so the cash must have been left there, on purpose or otherwise, before the snow started last night.

"Alexandria!" I seldom call her by her full name, so, on the rare occasions I do, she knows it's important."

"Yeah?"

"Come down. Right now. If you aren't dressed yet, bring your clothes and finish down here, but hurry. We need to talk."

Al pulled her shirt over her head and descended the stairs. "What's going on?"

"We've got a problem, and it's a big one." I pointed toward the ice cream container on the table. "Lift the lid a bit, but don't touch anything inside."

Al gasped, only the second true gasp I've heard in my life.

"But…How…Where…Who…How much?"

"I'm not sure. Maybe a hundred grand, more or less. Seamus found it this morning when he shoveled the neighbor's parking pad."

"What are we going to do?"

I stroked my beard and mustache for a moment. "This is probably criminal and, if so, they won't hesitate to kill the whole family to retrieve it. We need to get this back to the owners in a manner that's safe for us and them. I don't want anything to do with this money."

"Can't we keep some?"

"Are you serious? When's the last time you've seen a criminal cartel being given an award for humanitarian activities? Our safest bet may be to assure the owners that we have it safe for them and want to return it."

Al paced along the hallway. "Why don't we just put it back? Pretend we never saw the silly thing?"

"Good point. But how would we know the right people will end up with the package? We have to keep it safe and make sure the owners get it. I don't want to be awakened at oh-dark-thirty by someone who thinks we have what we don't. I especially don't want to be a tragic murder report where the whole family is wiped out, clear down to the last goldfish."

"Maybe we should call the police. If it's criminal, they'll want to know about it and, if it's not, we'll have an unblemished claim."

"The corruption probe, remember? It sounds like half the department is on the cartel's payroll. And even if they aren't, all we'd need is one cop with an overdue alimony payment to spill the beans on us. We wouldn't have the money, but the owner might want revenge for their reputation, if nothing else."

Al winced. "I'd forgotten the investigation."

"Right now, I don't trust the police and I'd rather not get them involved unless we have no choice. Besides, in terms of how it would impact us, calling the cops is no different from just leaving the package where we found it."

"Well, what do you want to do then? Hang a note from the window?"

"Like they'd be able to see—" My mouth stopped while my brain engaged. Unlike some people, I can't talk and think at the same time.

Al stopped her pacing and stared. "What?"

"Actually, that might not be a bad idea. Why don't you write one of those things that makes a computer do something?"

"A script? What for?"

"To make a series of repeating words go across a screen."

"A crawl? Our laptop isn't big enough to see from outside."

"No, we'll move our TV to the picture window and put the crawl on it. The words don't have to be fancy, maybe something like, I FOUND IT…I DON'T WANT IT…I HAVE IT SAFE FOR YOU…"

"You've lost your mind. How do you know the owner will come back here? And what if someone else sees the crawl and decides they want it? You have *got* to be certifiable."

"First of all, we're the last house on a dead end, remember? But even if we lived on a busy street, what would you think if you drove past a house and saw a message like this in a window? Would something that cryptic make you want to break in, intent on larceny?"

She said nothing for a moment. "OK, I'll give you that."

"Secondly, what do you do if you lose something? Retrace your steps, right?"

Al nodded.

"Only the person who lost it would follow their original path to come down our street where they could see a few simple words floating in our picture window and know the message applies to them." I took my glasses off and cleaned them while she thought. "Well, what's the verdict? Is there method in my madness?"

"I wish there was some other way."

"Me, too." I slipped my glasses back on. "So... Can you write a script for that crawl?"

"Shouldn't be too much trouble. Mind if I eat first?"

"What? Oh, yeah. I have coffee on, too." Al turned toward the kitchen, but I stopped her.

"Open the gun safe while you're there and get me the shoulder holster, would you please?"

Her eyes widened.

"I told you, this isn't a game. We shouldn't have any problems, but I don't want to take unnecessary risks."

I took the rig from her proffered hand and slid it on. People get the wrong idea about firearms and think they're like plastic toys. When I tell them wearing one is like wearing bricks in a harness, they don't believe me. TV and movies, I suppose.

Dropping the magazine, I checked the chamber. Clean and empty. What I'd expected, but I refuse to be negligent. I slid the magazine back into the weapon and, keeping it pointed toward a safe place, racked a round. Locked and loaded. I de-cocked the hammer, clicked the safety on, and slid the weapon back into the holster.

Should the worst happen, all I'd have to do would be pop off the safety and squeeze the trigger. Recoil would handle the following shots. I like shooting sports and make it a point to avoid shooting others. God willing, I won't have to start.

"Sweetie, I'm going to finish shoveling. If John's not up by the time you're done with breakfast, wake him. He can set up a table and help you move the tv."

***

Gulping a deep breath of air, I focused on the outdoor sounds. Only the traffic from the busy streets a few blocks away. I like the sound of snow being shoveled and it surprised me when I didn't hear anyone else. Were I the age of my sons, I'd view the silence as a business opportunity and work my way up and down the streets, but kids don't do that anymore.

Near the end of shoveling our side, I stopped and caught my breath. All the water in this snowfall made it really heavy and hard to move, which exacted a toll. On top of that, as the boys keep reminding me, I'm no spring chicken, so I have to pace myself and pay the toll man now and then.

A door slammed a few houses up the block and I raised my head. The mayor's daughter made her way down her steps while carrying a large trash bag.

I waved. "Morning, Donna! Looks like snow." It hadn't worked with Seamus, so I thought I'd try it on someone else.

She dropped the white kitchen bag into her dumpster and slammed the lid. "Oh, I dunno. You think?" she said and laughed.

Unable to tell if she was laughing at my wit or hers, I joined in. I've always tried to stay on good terms with all my neighbors, but especially her. All the city services get a little extra attention on our street, including snow removal, so being nice to her without being smothering was especially important. Sort of a balance between being obsequious and being neighborly.

She kicked some snow off her steps.

"And for heaven's sake, be careful. Do you want me to send the boys up with their shovels?"

"No, thanks. I'll get it in a little bit. See you later." She walked into her house and closed the door, leaving the quiet to flood back around me.

One more deep breath in and out, and I attacked the last portion of the pad. The effort brought the familiar sense of accomplishment, not unlike mowing a lawn, and I took a glance at it again as I leaned the snow shovel against the rosebush.

The snowplow would do a number on the work at the curb, but I wanted John to have some fun in the snow, i.e. sweat equity, too. Because of Donna, he wouldn't have to wait long. Besides, the work cleared my head, and I had a plan.

Al opened the door as I reached for the knob. I don't know how she does this, but it's happened more times than I can count. She told me once it just feels like I'm there and she wants to see me. That may be reason enough.

"Done? Already?"

Her smile warmed me more than coming indoors. I shut the door behind me and wrapped my arms around her. "Until the snowplow hits our street." I nodded toward John where he lounged in his customary spot on the loveseat. "Then it's his turn."

"My turn for what?" John raised his head.

"After the plow comes, I want the snow off the curb, especially on our neighbors' side. You need to do it as soon as it happens. Understand?"

"Aw, Dad." John is as informal as Seamus is formal. Same parents, same environment, but two different kids. Go figure.

"A long time ago, I had a chance to do something nice for someone who needed my help, but I didn't. I've regretted it ever since. Let's be a mensch whenever we get the chance. Got it?" I don't believe in asking for permission of my children and it grates my spine whenever I hear an adult do it, even if it's a simple 'OK?' at the end of a sentence.

John stared back into his tablet and mumbled.

"What?"

"I said, 'OK.' Geesh."

Al unzipped my coat. "I have the crawl done."

"Great. I need you to add something to it."

"Figures."

"It's simple, though. Just add, '*CHECK THE WINDSHIELD AT 10:00 p.m.*' to the end. I'm going to put some directions out there to keep them anonymous and us safe."

The snowplow rumbled down our side of the street, stopping at our dead end, backed up and did it again on the other side.

"John." I raised my voice. "John, they've played your song. Time to clear the curb."

My son shot me a venom-filled glance and rose from his loveseat. "Do I have to?"

"Seamus and I have already done our share. Man up, bud. You could be halfway done by now if you didn't argue."

"Nobody asked me if I wanted to."

"You're right, but all I have to do is make one call and your phone will be a boat anchor. Is that what you want?"

"No."

"And maybe you can spend the night with your cousins. How's that sound?"

John didn't answer. He rose, stretched, then bounded up the stairs, presumably to get dressed. I suppose nonverbal communication is still a reply.

"You didn't tell me anything about that."

"I'm sorry, Sweetie, it just occurred to me. Why don't you call your sister and see if you and the boys can spend the night? Just being prudent. Don't tell her about our dilemma, though. If she asks why, tell her we've hit a rocky patch and you three need to spend the night."

"Rocky patch? Listen to me, buster. If you think you're going to do all this cloak and dagger without me, you are sadly mistaken."

"There just isn't any need, Al."

"That is so lame. You need somebody to cover your back and I mean literally. What if they decide to take a shortcut and break in from the front and back at the same time? You can't handle anything like that alone."

Beautiful, brave, and brainy. That's what I married.

"OK, tell your sister it's an extra special date night and the boys are too old to stay home. Get her a pizza, too. They'll think it's a party." I pulled her into my arms and gave her a kiss and a strong hug. "Promise me you'll follow directions and stay safe."

She returned my hug and kissed me again. "No problem."

I slid out of her arms and sat at my computer. "I need to write up the instructions. Why don't you give your sister a call?"

***

The deadbolt jiggled and the front door swung open. I'd already unsnapped the safety strap on the shoulder holster when Al strode inside. "Hi, Sweetie." I re-snapped the strap and drew my hand out of the fleece. "Back already?"

She stopped short, her eyes wide. "Maybe I should've called first."

"You were never in any danger. How does the crawl look from the street?"

"Perfect. Are you done with the instructions?"

"For the most part. I'd like to see what you think before I print them." I rose from my chair and stretched. "And a bite to eat doesn't sound bad, either. Do you want to take a look while I make a toasted PB&J?"

"Really? For dinner?"

"Seamus had one for breakfast this morning, and it's been on my mind all day. With apricot preserves. Want one?"

"No thanks. I ate with the boys at Anne's."

"OK, then have a seat and start reading. Out loud, if you don't mind."

Al sat in my chair and cleared her throat. "*Season's Greetings.*" She scrunched up her nose. "Really?"

"I had to start somewhere. Keep going."

Al straightened her back. "*I found your package and don't want anything to do with it. I only brought it inside to keep it safe for you. Truth be known, I barely looked at it, then refastened the lid. All I want to do is give it back to you, the rightful owner.*"

"What do you think? How am I doing?"

"So far, so good. Stop interrupting." She took a deep breath. "*I don't want to know anything about you. Not about your car, not your license plate, and certainly not your appearance. Doubtless, the package contents were all legally obtained, but I want to be able to make a statement under penalty of perjury that I know nothing about you.*"

"Why are you stopping?"

"No reason. This just sounds so serious."

"It is. Deadly serious. People with this kind of money don't mess around, and I want to make sure everybody feels safe."

Al nodded. "*So, the problem becomes a simple one. How do I make sure you're the proper owner without seeing you or knowing anything about you? There is an answer. As we both know, your property came in a distinctive package.*"

"Clever, huh?"

"Very smart. *All you have to do is get another package, same brand, same flavor, same size, and put it on my front porch, next to the door at 12:15 am. Touch your horn twice, just a quick, beep, beep to let me know you've dropped off the duplicate container. I'll give you five minutes to leave the street before I get the empty package from the door."*

This was the important part. I stroked my mustache and beard, but kept my mouth shut.

She stared at the screen. *"I'll keep the lights on all evening which means I won't be able to see you, but you'll be able to see me. At 12:20 a.m., I'll turn off my lights, bring in the empty package, then turn them back on and compare containers. If everything matches, I'll turn off the lights at 12:30 a.m., just long enough to put your property outside my door, then turn everything back on in the house."*

I dabbed a stray bit of apricot preserves from the corner of my mouth with a paper towel. "If they do that, we'll be home free. Go ahead and finish up."

Al frowned. *"Check your property before you leave and make sure you have everything. Once you're satisfied, give me two quick beeps on your horn, followed by one more a few seconds later. A beep, beep... beep. We'll give you five minutes to leave before we turn out all our lights for the night."*

"So, what do you think?" I took a big slug of cold milk. "I should have worked for the CIA, right?"

She took that one lock of her hair behind her right ear and wrapped it around her little finger. I've seen her do that for years whenever she's thinking, and it's always her right, pinkie finger. I've never mentioned it, though. Al does this without the slightest hint of self-consciousness, and I want her to keep doing it that way. Just another thing about her to treasure.

"Not as good as you think." Al removed her finger from her hair. "You've given the owner all kinds of protection, but almost none for us."

"Yes, I did. I blacken the house before I open the door."

"It's not enough."

"What do you suggest?"

"The owner knows nothing about us, right?"

"Only where we live. Most likely, nothing else."

"So we could cook up any cock and bull story we want about our background and they'd have no way to verify it, would they?"

My internal light bulb turned on. Sometimes, I'll swear, I have the brains of a carrot.

"OK, how about adding this." I stroked my beard and mustache. "*I don't know anything about you and that's fine with me, so let's keep this peaceful. The authorities are only a three-digit phone call away, but I don't want to involve them.*"

Al nodded. "Good, so far. Keep it coming."

"*For all you know about me, I could have been a civilian contractor for the Army, teaching urban warfare and in-house combat with intra-room ambushes, but I'd like you to remember one thing. This is your property, and I don't want any of it. Not one bit. All you have to do is follow my suggestions and we both win. You have all your property and I get a peaceful night's sleep. Give me one quick tap on your car horn after you read this if the plan works for you.*"

She chuckled. "Urban warfare? Ambushes? Where do you come up with all this stuff?"

"Reality is just a place to start. Why don't you print that, and I'll get the carbine and put it in the bathroom?"

"The bathroom?"

"Yup. You said you were going to cover my back and that's as far back as the house goes."

"The bathroom?"

My voice took on an unaccustomed note of exasperation. "Yes, Alexandre-e-e-e-a, the bathroom." She hates it when I stretch out her name like that, so I only do it when I need to take a point and rub it in. "Anyone coming in from the back door has to pass that bathroom, so it's the perfect place to stop them. Sit in a lawn chair and use the navy-blue blanket to cover yourself and the chair. Keep the door half open, and the light difference will make you invisible."

She gave me a stony look, but I didn't stop.

"You said you'd follow my directions. Well, from 9:55 this evening until ten minutes after the final exchange, you're covering my back from the bathroom. Lock and load when you get in there."

"Can I watch a video?"

"Nope. The light would give you away. You can listen to a book, but only on one earbud. If someone tries to break in, you need to be able to hear. Get a lawn chair and wear your darkest clothes." I pulled the carbine from the gun safe and, since we don't store this weapon with a loaded magazine, went through an abbreviated safety check. She'd know what to do.

***

Al slid the magazine into her weapon and cycled the action, the sound clearly audible from her place in the bathroom. Normally, I wouldn't find this bothersome, but we'd never set out with the intent to defend hearth and home before. This one evening, however, the thought sobered me.

"Don't forget—"

"Yes, yes, I know," she said. "Safety off and trigger discipline."

"We'd better quit talking. I don't want them discovering you if they come early. In case you don't hear the horn, don't talk to me again until I talk to you." I reached into my shoulder holster and clicked off the safety. What's good for the goose…

"OK," she said. "Love you."

Did her voice just quiver?

"Love you, too. Bunches. This will all be over in a heartbeat and everything will be all right."

She didn't answer, but I didn't expect her to. I checked the time on my phone. 9:57.

Waiting sucks.

Rather than use my computer, I pulled up a social media account on my phone and scrolled down. Pictures and text rolled under my finger, but I didn't pay much attention. I like to write and may have been too smart by half when I came up with these instructions. Just one more thing to worry me.

A car horn beeped outside, just one quick tap, and I relaxed. Thank God. Five minutes after I pulled up the timer app, it went off in a series of harmonious tones.

"Well," Al said from her position as rear guard. "Did they bite?"

"It's too soon to tell, but the signs are good." I flicked the safety back on. "Why don't you clear the carbine and leave it in there? I need your help out here."

She came out of the bathroom wearing my Mossy Oak fleece with a turkey hunter's see-through facemask. "This thing itches. I don't see how you can stand it. What's up?"

"I need your help getting the TV back in the entertainment center and putting the table away. I think we're done with the HDMI cable, too, so you can stop your laptop, as well."

"What next?"

"We wait. I gave the owner a couple hours to get and clean an identical container, so you don't need to get back on station until about midnight."

"Good." Al took off my fleece and tossed it on a chair. "At least I can be comfortable."

"You don't need to wear it. You could use something of your own."

"Yeah, I do. Nothing I have looks so good in the dark."

"Were you admiring yourself in the mirror?"

"I had to make sure it would work."

"Can't argue with that, I suppose." I yawned. "How about I make us some cocoa after we get things put away?" I love hot chocolate, but most people make it so thin, it's hard for me to taste. More often than not, I quadruple the amount of chocolate, so I don't make it very often. I wonder if a ground dark chocolate would have a good enough flavor to let me use less.

"OK, but don't make mine as strong as yours." She stopped the crawl and folded her laptop. "Give me a hand with the TV."

***

Al glanced at her phone. "I guess it's about showtime. I'd better go back and guard the garderobe."

"Oh, aren't you the brilliant one?"

"Well, our home is our castle, right? It seemed to fit."

Her words showed her nervousness as much as her wit. In a few minutes, we'd know where we stood. Or lay. I grimaced. *Why do I have to think like that?* Instead, I focused on what we'd done. We'd even scrubbed the outside of the container with dish soap while wearing exam gloves, making sure we left no trace of ourselves on the surface.

A car horn sounded twice in front of our home, and I pulled up my phone's timer app again. Five more minutes. I hadn't threatened the owner with police involvement on purpose, but what if the container was wrong? Calling the authorities was always my backup plan, but I hoped I wouldn't have to resort to it. I slipped on a pair of exam gloves.

The familiar tones sounded again, and I silenced the alarm. "Time to blackout, Al," I said, but she didn't answer. I turned out all the lights and approached the front door, then pulled it open. My façade is brick, so I felt safe standing next to the doorway. Not so much the glass storm door, though. Lowering myself to my knees where I stood, I opened the storm door and dragged the container inside by the handle.

I'd already started the timer app when I turned out the lights, so I forced myself upright, leaning against the wall, my heart going ninety miles a minute. I jumped when the alarm tones went off again.

"OK, I'm turning on the lights, now, sweetie. Stay there while I check things out." I blinked in the sudden brightness, then focused on the two containers. Same brand, same gallon size, same chocolate vanilla swirl flavor. I released a big breath I didn't remember holding.

"Looks like this guy's the owner, gorgeous."

My angel said nothing, but I could imagine her relief.

"Two minutes 'til blackout, and we'll be done with this whole thing." I strode to the light switch, still wearing the exam gloves and holding the original container. This time, I stopped the app before it sounded and turned off the lights again.

This was it. We hadn't touched the contents, but what if someone else had? I forced the doubt from my mind, opened the front door one last time, and studied my yard. Clear. Going down to my knees again, I opened the storm door and lowered the container with all the money in it onto the porch then closed and locked both doors, my heart beating so fast I thought it might explode.

"It's out of the house, Al."

When the timer app went off again, I walked about, turning on each light. I went back to my seat where I could be easily seen and scrolled through social media on my phone. Normally, I prefer to use my laptop because the keyboard makes it easier to reply, but I wanted to be able to face the door. Of course, one of the reasons I used my phone was I'd have it in my hands if I needed to call the police. Just in case.

I didn't notice the pictures or text as they flew by under my fingers. Listening took more of my attention than the images on my phone, and I thought I'd never hear another car horn.

But I heard it. Beep, beep... Beep. I took a deep breath. Five more minutes to let them leave, and we'd be free. "Al, they got it all."

"Can I come out?"

"Not yet. In... um, four more minutes, I'm going to turn out the lights. That's the last sign."

"Did we really pull this off?"

"Looks like it. How do you feel?"

"Like I want to cry."

"I know what you mean."

I wasn't speaking idly. A couple years earlier, she'd had a bad infection that resulted in blood sepsis. The ER nurse had made a casual statement about transporting her to another hospital, depending on the test result. When the test came back negative, I was so relieved, I cried. This surprised me. I'd seen movies and heard of people who'd broken into tears of relief all my life. I never thought it would happen to me, though.

I rose and turned out the lights. "Olly, olly oxen free."

Al came out of the bathroom. "What did you say?"

"It feels like we've reached home base and everything's clear."

"Maybe not. They may have some sort of code or honor thing they think they have to uphold. What do you think about staying up and keeping armed for another couple hours or so?"

"See what I mean? I tell people all the time, I married up to you. You are not only beautiful, you're smart, too. That's a great idea."

"What do you want to do while we wait?"

"If we could have lights on, I'd suggest a game of hand and foot."

"That does sound good." Al wrapped her pinky finger in her hair. "But maybe we should keep in the dark. Shows trust."

"You know what? I like talking with you. What do you say we just chat for a couple of hours?"

She unwrapped her finger. "Sure. We can do that."

***

At close to three o'clock, Al yawned. "I'm getting tired. What do you think?"

My reciprocal yawn couldn't be stopped. "You know what honest crooks and honest politicians have in common?"

"No, what?"

"They stay bought."

Al barked a short laugh and cleared the carbine. "I can't tell you how glad I am that we didn't have to use these." She put the carbine into the gun safe and held out her hand for the shoulder holster.

"Me, too." I cleared the automatic and handed the rig to her.

She hung up the shoulder holster, closed the door and spun the lock. "I wonder if it's snowing."

"I'd heard it might."

Al opened the front door. "What's this?" She pointed to an envelope taped to the other side of the glass.

"I don't know, but don't touch it."

"What? Why not?"

"If it's from the owner, which seems likely, I don't want any of his DNA inside the house. And don't tell me I'm being ridiculous. When I was in tenth grade, we were able to bring up fingerprints on paper. If they could do it all those years ago, think what they could do now with DNA. Wait a minute." I went to the table and pulled out a couple exam gloves. "Here, put these on. Stay outside, too. I don't want any trace of the owner in our home."

"We already have his ice cream container in here."

"We'll scrub it later and stick it in the bottom of the trash."

Al slid the exam gloves onto her hands and pulled the envelope off the door, then stepped into the light. "On the outside, it says, 'It's a pleasure doing business with honorable people. Consider this a finder's fee.' Can I open it, now?" She didn't wait for an answer but tore the flap and lifted a printed greeting. "It's a Christmas card." She opened it. "With money. Hundred-dollar bills. Ten of them."

"Damn hell, you say! A whole grand?" A tremor of 1 on the Richter scale could have knocked me off balance at that moment, but none came and, with a deep breath or two, I kept upright. "What's on the card?"

"Let me see… 'May the peace of this Christmas season be yours now and throughout the coming year.' That's nice." She said nothing for a moment. "I think we're safe. They could have given us anything or nothing, but they chose one that emphasized peace."

"You may be right, but I don't want to take chances. Stay outside. I'll be right there." I strode to the kitchen and pulled a lighter out of the counter along with some window cleaner and a paper towel.

"Hurry up, it's started snowing again."

I grabbed her coat after I slid mine on and stepped through the door.

"It's about time."

"Oh, quit your bellyaching." I draped her coat over her shoulders and placed the hood over her head.

She sighed. "I think you're carrying this thing too far."

"I'm afraid of the police as much as I am of the owner. If the cops are as crooked as the investigation reports on the news say, the boys in blue would use anything as an excuse to make our lives miserable. I'm probably overreacting, but I don't want to give them any reason."

"Still, you may have been reading too many crime and spy novels."

"Maybe. Or I'm just being prudent." I took the snow shovel and scooped some snow down to the frozen dirt from the pile beside the sidewalk, then laid the shovel on the sidewalk behind me, careful to keep all the snow on the shovel. "OK, give me the money."

Al responded with a light chuckle. "Now you sound like a movie."

"Ha, ha. Did you get the tape from the storm door, too?"

"Yep. There wasn't much, so I just wrapped it around the envelope." She opened the card and handed one thousand dollars to me. "Hmm… We should check these out and make sure they're not counterfeit. Do you know how to do it?"

"No, but we'll be able to find something on the internet in the morning. If they're all OK, we'll take everybody, including Anne and her family, out for a meal at that fancy breakfast and lunch place." I slid the money into my coat pocket.

"Now what?"

"Take the card out and hold it over the bare spot." I picked up a small stick and broke it to a point, then held out the blunt end to her. "Take off one exam glove, hold the stick with your bare hand, and stab it through the card but not far. I'm going to burn it, so hold it over the bare spot."

"Shouldn't we have marshmallows?" she said and pushed the stick through the Christmas greeting.

"Oh, you are such a wit tonight." I pulled out the lighter, squatted down and set the flame to the card. After a minute or two, only ashes remained.

"Same plan for the envelope?"
"Yup."

In a moment's time, the ashes of the envelope joined those of the card, but I waited until the last embers died.

"Are we done yet?"

"Almost. Stir the ashes with the stick for a minute. That way, nobody will be able to identify them by shape."

When she finished, I picked up the snow shovel and covered the scattered ashes with the snow Seamus had piled up in the morning. "If it snows enough tonight to shovel in the morning, no one, but no one will be able to tell we did anything."

"What shall I do with the gloves?"

"Glad you mentioned it. Did they both turn inside out when you took them off?"

"Yes."

"Great. Stuff one inside the other, then give them to me. I'll put them in the dumpster of the mayor's daughter. I saw her drop in a trash bag just before I came inside from shoveling, and I'll stuff it in there." I pulled the napkin and glass cleaner from my coat. "Why don't you clean the storm door, then go in and warm up? I'll be back in a trice."

On my round trip to Donna's dumpster, I ran over a contingency plan. What if, after all our efforts and care, the detectives came to our door wanting information? After I planted the gloves inside the trash bag and gently lowered the lid, I knew the answer. Tell the truth. Obstruction of justice? How could we have known? I smiled at the elegance of the idea as I approached our porch. Simple. Just like returning a lost puppy.

As soon as I stepped up to our door, Al opened it again. I wish I knew how she can tell when I reach for the door. It's solid without so much as a peephole, but she still opens it before I can.

"Thanks, you beautiful, gorgeous thing." I stepped inside, took off my coat and tossed it over a chair. "Are you ready for bed yet, or do we need to do something else exciting? Rob a gold shipment or a bank somewhere?"

Al gave me a sly grin. "I told Anne that we had a really hot date night planned. You wouldn't want to make a liar of me, would you?"

I closed and locked the front door, then slid my arms around her, pulling her tight. "You'll be a paragon of virtue."

--William R. Bartlett is retired from the insurance industry and currently writes the *Word from Dad* feature in Kansas City Parent magazine, which he's done since the April 2009 issue. A lifelong resident of the Kansas City area and no stranger to snow, he's currently putting the finishing touches on a romance novel, *Nude, Light Housekeeping*.

America, The Not So Beautiful
By Robin Cain

"America! America! God shed His grace on thee. And crown thy good with brotherhood, from sea to shining sea!"[1]

Some old man on the street, singing a song on one bent knee. How was I to know if he had directed it at me? I wasn't about to grant him any attention when just the sight of him caused me great apprehension.

Suddenly he began yelling. "Winter is on its way!"

I only knew that I needed to leave without delay. I'd heard that homeless people were constantly smoking meth. Please let me pass by unharmed, I prayed, nearly out of breath.

"Hey lady, I mean you no harm," he said. "I just hoped my song might earn me some bread."

He'd called to me from his camp under a roadside bridge, hunkered down all alone beside a rusty old fridge. I couldn't ignore him, for he was less than ten feet from me, and shivering in the damp cold with no coat that I could see. His hands were gnarled with age, his face awash in dirt. He wore pants full of holes and a thin, long sleeve shirt. His worn-out shoes spoke of the miles he had most likely traveled, the soles missing rubber and laces completely unraveled.

He now had my attention. He'd piqued my curiosity. But I'd be brief, fearing my words would promote reciprocity.

"Goodness, aren't you cold?"

"Yes…if truth be told."

There was really nothing in his manner to give me any pause and, having now seen his plight, I needed to determine its cause.

I cautiously stepped from the safety of the sidewalk and asked him kindly for his name.

"Alex P Dorn, III," he said proudly, as if the extra title would fend off shame. "But I'd prefer you to just call me Pete. That's been my name since my feet hit the street."

"How long have you lived here?" I asked, surveying his sad, worn-out tent.

"Just a few weeks. My last place was destroyed by the cops that were sent. No damn compassion from anyone. We are now all just strays. Seems the world has become a harsh, unforgiving place these days."

When I asked what he had done in his previous life, all he could tell me was how much he missed his dear wife. She'd kicked him out when he couldn't control this desire to drink, and everything he once knew seemed to vanish in a blink. He'd lost his job due to uncontrollable depression, then the country experienced a massive recession. In those months that followed, he traversed the city, sideways and back. There was no place like home, but he knew he'd never be welcomed back.

With his money running short and no roof over his head, what was left of any optimism soon turned to dread.

Then the day came when he realized he had to stop being proud so he went in search of corners where panhandling might be allowed. He'd hold out his hand for a dollar or two, but generous strangers were just far too few.

Get off the streets, they would tell him. Go get yourself a job. As if he could just stroll into the local Charles Schwab™.

Now he stood shivering in the hard cold next to me, owned a poor excuse of a house that required no key. He turned his gaze to the little diner across the street, asked if I thought they would be kind, give him something to eat.

In that instant, I compared his life to mine. Our paths crossing was surely some kind of sign. How does a man end up homeless on the street, with no easy way to get back on his feet? What would I do if this happened to me? How many people would answer my plea?

The answers made my insides ache. How much could a man really take?

I quickly rummaged inside my new designer purse, found a wad of cash that now suddenly seemed perverse.

"Let's get out of here and find you some food," I suggested, though I thought it an idea he might have protested.

"You say you're willing to eat with me, my friend. My shoddy appearance might surely offend. You are standing here dressed in such fine clean clothes, and this might matter to others, heaven knows."

"People will always find a way to cast stones. Winter's coming, and you need meat on your bones. I have never walked in your shoes nor felt your pain. It's time I looked after others and not complain."

He caught his breath and stood beside a big oak tree, stretched himself to the height of a man newly free.

"Winter is coming indeed," he agreed. "But I asked for nothing, showed you no greed. I could use food in my belly and a shelter that is secure. I'm a homeless man and far from rich, but this is just a detour. Given some time, I know I will get back on my feet, and I'll no longer be a man living on the street."

"So just for right now, let me buy you a meal, and maybe a warm coat as part of the deal. But we'd better hurry before it gets too late." Then I held up a hand to stay future debate.

We walked to the diner and ordered something to eat, ignoring the looks of others that were none too discreet. We talked for hours and hours over hot soup and bread, both of us imagining better days ahead.

Once we had finished our meal and I paid the small bill, he thoughtfully thanked me for what he deemed my goodwill.

"I've spent many a day hungry, cold, and alone on the street. There was never any compassion in the strangers I'd meet. For a long, long while, I wondered where kindness had been, but you've made me believe in humanity again. Although the dark days of winter are already here, I now may survive and see Spring in the coming year."

He stopped for a moment and scratched his scraggly beard, but the light in his eyes suddenly disappeared. "Now please tell me what I can possibly do for you in return. You don't seem to have any visible needs that I can discern."

"No human should starve, be left out in the cold. These are things we were taught, things we were told. All basic rights we should try to uphold. I have all I need, Alex P. Dorn, III. It is you who do not. And it is only by the grace of God that I do not share your spot. You've taught me that things aren't what they seem at first glance. Our paths crossing today was surely happenstance.

"A kind of winter lies ahead for all of us, we just know not to what degree. It's time we band together and end our selfishness. It's an easy recipe. A good meal, a few dollars, and a warm coat could be just enough to keep one man afloat. Sharing one's fortune should be our new creed, not only in thought but also through deed. The lyrics that you shared with me had the right intention. The humans of this country just need an intervention. It's high time we look after one another. Treat everyone as if he were our brother."

I hadn't intended to make such a decree, but then…

Alex P. Dorn, III, belted out those lyrics again.

"America! America! God shed His grace on thee. And crown thy good with brotherhood…from sea to shining sea.[1]"

Caught up as I was in my impromptu speech, then the homeless man's song, I hadn't realized that the room had been following all along. But one by one, the other diners stood and began to applaud, convincing me that maybe our righteous ideas weren't so flawed.

[1]Katharine Lee Bates, Lyrics to "America The Beautiful", 1895

--Robin Cain is the author of *When Dreams Bleed* and *The Secret Miss Rabbit Kept*. A Midwest girl who never much liked the snow and the cold so aptly described in these pages, Robin currently resides in Scottsdale, AZ. When not writing or editing, she's likely wandering—because that's where all the great stories live. Robin can be reached at <u>robin@robincain.com</u>

The Last Door

By Chris Stenson

Billy rolled over and hit snooze. His dog, Arlo, jumped on the bed, licked his face with reckless abandon, urging him out of bed. He playfully swatted Arlo and rubbed his head. "Enough. I know what time it is."

Outside, the snow swirled into large pillowy drifts. Maybe school would be canceled today?

He gathered his winter gear and proceeded to get dressed as Arlo's tail waved in anticipation. He gazed at his dog. "I'm hurrying."

At the door, Arlo planted his butt on the tile floor before being asked.

"Such a good boy."

Billy snapped on the lead and they went outside. The cold bit his cheeks. He wanted to go back inside and crawl under the covers before they reached the end of the driveway.

They approached the pond. The wind howled into their faces and snow pellets obscured their vision. Arlo found fresh tracks. His short stub of a tail wagged faster, and they picked up the pace. They found their nemesis--a small, dark gray shadow sat nervously at the edge of the pond.

Arlo whimpered and pulled hard at the lead. Billy laughed at the look his dog gave him.

"Okay. Okay. I understand." Billy gave his best friend a hug and unsnapped the lead. "Do you think you can catch him today?"

The chase was on.

The pair zig-zagged across the fresh snow. Every time Arlo got close, the rabbit dialed up the speed, keeping a safe distance between them. Billy cheered his dog on, knowing that he would never catch the speedy hare.

The jackrabbit, with Arlo close behind, disappeared into the six-foot-high black maw that led under the road and to the pond on the other side. Arlo made a surprised yelp, and the early morning became uncomfortably silent.

The quiet scared Billy. He raced to the tunnel, following the only tracks in the freshly fallen snow.

"Arlo?"

Billy scrambled to the other side of the road, but no tracks exited. He had no choice. His best friend had disappeared. He crossed back over and stood in front of the blackness. He shivered and pounded his boots against the frozen pond. The cold had seeped beneath his clothing and a chill radiated throughout his body. "Arlo. Arlo. Are you in there?"

His chest tightened and he took a couple of hesitant steps forward. What if a coyote was hiding in the darkness or there was an area of thin ice Amos had fallen through? Pulling up his big boy pants and swallowing his fear, Billy stepped into the darkness The faint light from the surrounding streetlamps leaked in and allowed him to see. The tunnel wasn't as claustrophobic as he imagined it to be. A simple, but large culvert. The tracks ended in front of a door drawn on the tunnel wall. He ran his hand, not over a cement wall, but a wood grained surface. "What the hell?" He grabbed the cold metal door handle and pulled. Did he believe Arlo had disappeared through a door drawn with Magic Markers?

He stumbled backwards. "Arlo."

Wiping his arm across his face, Billy turned to run, but tripped. He scrambled to his knees. Brushing away the snow with his hand, he uncovered a door frozen in the ice, its corner protruding from the surface of the pond. He stopped at the entrance and scratched his head. Who would dispose of a door here?

"Arlo. Arlo. Where are you boy?"

Billy limped outside into the growing winter storm. The wind buffeted his back and he trudged home, calling for Arlo after every couple of steps, tears frozen at the corner of his eyes.

The temperature continued to plummet, and the snow drifted and piled up everywhere. Billy sat by the windows for two days and waited. After each wind gust rattled the house, he rushed to the door and threw it open, expecting Arlo to be sitting on the front stoop. Every time his dog wasn't there, the pain and loss gripped Billy tighter. He begged his parents to let him go searching, but their answer was always the same — after the storm ended.

Once he had shoveled the sidewalks, Billy hurried to the pond. Scrubbed blue ice and large snow waves covered the surface. Out of the corner of his eye, he sensed movement. He stopped and scanned the horizon. A face appeared under the ice then disappeared. Another step, another face. What the hell? He picked up his pace. The faces disappeared under a drift then came into view again.

The snow crunched under Billy's feet as he hurried to the tunnel. Several footprints stopped at the edge of the shadows and led back to the drawn door. He stood in the darkness and listened to a dog barking on the other side. The frantic, scared cries of Arlo. Tears stung Billy's cold cheeks.

He inspected the other door, the one frozen in the ice. Scratched into the frost were the words, 'Find the key'. This was the way in. If he wanted to save Arlo, he would need to find the key. Standing too close to the drawn door brought horrible thoughts and nightmare visions. He suspected black magic opened that door.

Billy walked the neighborhood and the places that he and Arlo loved to visit the most. His friend was kidnapped, trapped in another world. At home, his parents promised they would help search for his dog.

The next day, family and friends searched in vain, knocking on doors and plastering light poles with pictures of Arlo. When dusk settled and the temperature dropped back below zero, Billy ran home, slammed the door to his room, and collapsed onto his bed, angry and dejected. His mother said she would call the pound again the next day. Billy appreciated all the help, but he needed to find the key. If he told anyone that his dog Arlo had disappeared through a door drawn with a Magic Marker, they would think he had fluff for brains.

The sunshine was deceiving. The afternoon temperature hovered around minus ten, and sundogs encircled the sun. Bundled in multiple layers and holding a fistful of flyers, Billy left the house in search of Arlo. He placed a few of the missing posters into mailboxes and hurried towards the pond. The wind had turned direction and snow fell.

Billy tromped through the growing snow drifts and the ever-changing landscape, making a beeline across the pond. The snow fell faster and heavier the closer he got. The black maw of the tunnel became lost in a misty vagueness. A girl with glowing green eyes stood at the entrance but ducked into the tunnel when he approached. He clenched his fists, and with his chest heaving, he hurried forward. The wind rushed overhead, but the inside of the tunnel was comparatively quiet and free of snow. The outline of the drawn door glowed. Billy sat down hard on the ice and shivered as the wild storm raged outside.

A river of emotions flooded Billy when he considered the possibilities of the two doors. Evil hid behind the drawn one, waiting to steal innocent souls. The door frozen in the ice was his way in and would lead him to Arlo. He pressed his ear to the wood and listened.

Billy's frustration finally boiled over. He pounded on the door with gloved hands. After each blow, his breath exploded into a cascading white fog. His eyelashes frozen together with tears, he slumped against the door. "I must have done something wrong. Tell me what I did or how I sinned. I want my dog. Give me Arlo."

Billy sat in the eerie silence. Outside the tunnel, the wind moaned, the snow swirled and drifted at the entrance. Underneath the clear ice, shadows too big to be sunfish or bullheads, darted in the depths. A lifeless face peered up at him, hands pressed against the ice. Billy stood. Nothing would stop him. He was determined to find his dog at all costs.

The next morning, Billy hid his father's axe in his backpack before leaving for school. He had one stop to make before the bell rang. As he stepped onto the pond, the cold bit into his cheeks and watered his eyes. Another frigid day in the north country. His dog's nemesis had returned.

"Where's Arlo?" Billy asked the jackrabbit when it appeared before him.

The jackrabbit's ears perked up for a second before it bounded away. Billy took out the axe and followed across the snow-covered pond.

The girl with the green eyes stood in front of the dark opening of the tunnel, her skirt billowing in the harsh wind. She smiled. "He likes beautiful children."

Billy brandished the axe in a threatening manner. "I want Arlo back."

"Silly boy." she said.

"Who are you?"

"I'm a Collector."

"A collector of what?"

"Childrens souls."

Billy's mouth fell open and he stumbled forward. "Holy shit."

She laughed and, in a swirl of snow, disappeared into the tunnel.

When Billy stepped into the darkness, the outline of the drawn door glowed a poisonous green color. He didn't care. He dropped to the snow and chopped at the corner of the other door, hoping to free it from the ice. Chips of ice flew in all directions, covering his jacket in a thin layer of sparkling crystals. He made little progress. A small headache bloomed.

Billy clutched his head, but that didn't stop the random visions of dead children, their haunting vacant stares, nor the malevolent words they whispered. He gripped the handle tighter and chopped harder. "Leave me alone."

Crying, he shoved the axe into his backpack and escaped the darkness of the tunnel, determined they wouldn't win.

The winter dragged on. Some mornings, Billy would stand outside the tunnel and listen to Arlo bark. He was lost without his dog. His parents promised to buy him a new best friend for his birthday, but he didn't want a new dog. He hoped for an early spring so that the pond ice would melt and the door would open. He was sure that was the answer.

The headaches became more frequent. His daydreams were interrupted by dark thoughts and whispered voices. The children followed him everywhere, hiding in the shadows, and giving him brief glimpses of their faces so he wouldn't forget. Sleep came in short, restless bursts. The children and the nightmares were wearing him down. His soul was tired.

His mother sat at the edge of his bed every night, kissed his forehead, and tucked the blankets under his chin. One evening, she said, "I know you miss Arlo. We all miss your crazy dog. Try and get some sleep tonight. Your dad and I are getting worried."

Billy tried, but his dreams were vivid. He fought to stay awake.

The girl with the green eyes held Billy's severed head. "He likes beautiful children."

"He does, Billy," said a priest with black eyes.

"The Dark Ones are demons who have been waiting patiently for the darkness to return. Their time is approaching fast. They survive by drinking the blood of the innocent. They want to devour your soul," the priest said.

Billy tried to curtail the scream, but his fear overwhelmed his brain.

His eyes snapped open.

The blank faces of the pond children stared at him through his bedroom window. Billy's mind screamed. He lashed out, flinging his arm and legs, kicking his covers to the floor. He woke in a cold sweat, buried his head in his pillow, and wept.

At breakfast, his dad commented about his shoddy appearance, the unruly hair, the dark circles under his eyes, and his wrinkled clothes. Did they need to see a doctor?

Billy chewed and swallowed. Chewed and swallowed. Where would he start? The dead children staring into his room every night or the girl with the green eyes who drew magic-marker doors and walked through them? Better yet, maybe he should tell them about the priest with the midnight-black eyes who visited his dream last night. The priest told him about the Dark Ones, ancient demons who ate children's souls and how they wanted his.

"I'm fine."

Before the interrogation continued, a girl wearing a long vintage wool coat and leading a dog, walked past their dining room window. She wouldn't be that brazen, would she?

"Billy, are you listening to us?" His mother asked.

A few minutes later, the girl with the green eyes knelt and hugged the dog— his dog. She waved at him, smiled, and disappeared.

Billy dropped his cereal spoon and rushed outside. "Arlo?" he called. Mean and violent thoughts filled his mind.

The girl and the dog stopped and turned. Arlo bared his fangs. A growl from deep within warned Billy not to take another step.

"Why are you doing this?"

"Because I can," said the girl with the green eyes.

Billy scrambled after them, almost running just to keep up. He dared not to follow too close, or Arlo would snap and growl. What had this witch done to his dog?

At the pond, the jackrabbit warren had grown to five overnight. Four of his classmates hadn't been in class the last week and some of the kids were whispering at school about their disappearance. Were they turning school children into rabbits?

When the girl and the dog entered the tunnel, the girl pulled out an ancient-looking bronze key from her coat pocket and inserted it into the drawn door. When door swung open evil wafted out in waves. A swirling mist of shapes and shadows, twisting and stretching, leaching the warmth and color from what ever surface it touched. Billy wrinkled his nose. The smell of decay, of rotted meat, of earthy dead things, filled the small space.

The girl turned to Billy. "Do you want to come in?"

Billy took a step forward. The cloud snatched at his arm, he stumbled. "I…"

The girl pushed the door open wider. "Arlo misses you. He wants to play."

Arlo barked. His tail wagged and he bounced up and down as if excited to play, but his eyes gleamed with hatred. They had turned his best friend into some kind of monster.

With tears in his eyes, Billy shuffled closer. He grabbed his head, trying to stop the moaning and wailing voices vibrating inside his skull. "I don't want to die."

The girl laughed. "Death isn't forever." She stepped through the doorway and Arlo followed.

Shivering, Billy wrapped his arms around himself and headed home.

Every morning before school, no matter the temperature or weather conditions, Billy attacked the ice holding the partially submerged door hostage. The voices, the threats, and the headaches intensified. He made little progress, but he wouldn't give up on rescuing Arlo.

One morning, his parents ambushed him at the bottom of the stairs.

"We're getting concerned."

Billy shrugged.

"Are you drinking? Doing drugs?"

Billy shook his head.

"Is it a girl?"

Billy laughed. If they meant the poison-eyed bitch that took Arlo, then yes. "What a load of shit. I need to go."

"You can't speak to us that way," his mother said.

He pushed his way past them, put on his winter outer gear, and left. He had a hole to chop.

"Where are you going?"

He slammed the door.

***

Billy had to pee, bad. He crawled out of bed and stepped into the dimly lit hallway. A silent emptiness surrounded him. A small, pale white figure stood at the end of the hall.

"Hello, Billy."

The unnatural sound of the voice chilled him. Clear, feminine, and diabolically sweet.

A cold, sharp blade was pressed against his Achilles tendon. Billy choked down a scream. More eyes appeared in the shadows of the hallway. Standing with her hand on his parents' door, the girl with green eyes smiled. Soft footfalls sounded on the stairs. He was being hunted by a band of dead children and their master.

"What do you want?" Billy screamed.

"Your soul," they said in unison. "Come play with us."

Billy shivered.

The nightmares had escalated. The dead children now invaded his home nightly, the girl flaunted Arlo daily, and the priest with the black eyes hid in every shadow. The pond ice had broken apart the previous day and, overnight, the pieces had washed ashore. The time had arrived. The waiting was over. He would open the door and take the battle to them.

Billy had collected old keys all winter by visiting pawn shops and antique stores. He had searched online markets and paid for ads with his allowance. His collection was impressive. One of the keys would open the abandoned door. He was certain of it. He would take back his sanity.

That night, before going to bed, he opened his closet to put his clean clothes away and found a door drawn on the back wall of his closet. The green-eyed witch had been in his room. They were coming to get him. He cowered in the corner. Whispers and taunts filled the tiny space. He pushed his dresser in front of his closet and locked the door, but would that stop anyone from entering his room?

He was scared shitless.

Arlo whined and scratched at the closet door. Billy laid in bed, clutching his axe, expecting his dresser to topple, and all the creatures the girl controlled to escape. He would never reach safety in time. The green-eyed girl warned him that someone had to die—either him or one of his parents.

Billy crawled out of bed and opened his bedroom door. One of the dead children stood in the hallway.

"He's coming for you."

Fear pierced Billy's heart like a dart. His legs wobbling, he grabbed the door for support.

"You'll be one of us." The dead girl smiled. "Which parent do I get to kill?"

Behind the closet door, the voices were silent, and Arlo no longer whined.

Billy's pulse raced. His lips trembled. He bolted downstairs to the front door. He unlocked it and shook it, but the door wouldn't open.

"You're not leaving," the young child said. "She won't let you."

Billy clapped his hands over his ears to drown out the words. When he leaned against the door, his breath came out in short, raspy bursts. He needed to find a way out. The garage. He would try escaping through the garage.

He tried the garage door opener time and time again, then tossed the useless device on the floor. Using his arm, he wiped the sweat from his forehead.

Think, Billy, think.

Someone knocked on the door Billy stood against. "Let me in, let me in."

The sound of children's laughter surrounding him, Billy searched the garage until he found the tackle boxes and the filet knife. He ran his thumb along the edge, smiled, and folded his weapon. Do dead children bleed?

He inched open the door into the house, the knife clutched in a white-knuckle grip, but silence and darkness greeted him. He made his way to his room and crawled into bed unscathed.

***

Billy woke to an uncomfortable silence. With his heart racing, he jumped out of bed. Someone, or something, had moved the dresser from in front of the closet door. Muddy paw prints lead to his parent's bedroom door where bug-infested water pooled.

"Mom? Dad?"

Silence.

This wasn't good.

Billy stood in front of his parents' door, drenched in apprehension and fear. He didn't pray often enough or pay as much attention in church as he should, but this next request was important.

"Please be there." He took a deep breath and turned the knob. "Mom. Dad. Are you…?"

Droplets of blood covered the bedsheets and a crimson trail led to the closet. A wave of dizziness passed over Billy. His legs growing weak, he crumbled to the floor. He clutched his head in his hands. "Why me? Why did you choose me?"

He needed proof that the girl with the green eyes had kidnapped or killed his parents. No one would believe that she had transported them through a Magic Marker portal to another world.

He opened their closet door. Another drawn door, and a mirror showed his parents dangling from the gallows. Written above the doorway were the words: *We Chose for You.* With his stomach churning, he backed away in quick, jerky steps. Today, he would plunge into the icy waters to rescue Arlo and his parents.

***

Transparent blocks of honeycombed ice dotted the surface of the pond. When Billy stepped forward a shiver ran unchecked through his body. He took another tentative step and gritted his teeth. His feet were already numb, but he only had one shot to unlock the partially submerged door, find his parents, and rescue Arlo. He stumbled towards a final confrontation with the green-eyed girl and the dead children.

Despite chattering teeth and fingers that felt like frozen sausages, Billy tiptoed into the icy water of the pond, the keys to unlock the submerged door stuck in his front pockets. The few keys he retrieved slipped from his numb fingers and now sparkled on the bottom.

"Just great," Billy said as the last of the keys sank. "God damn hands."

He didn't have much time left before hypothermia set in. He took a deep breath and plunged underwater. Children taunted him with cruel whispers. He kicked harder towards the glint on the bottom. He scooped a handful of keys and tried to resurface.

A pale face appeared in front of him, and invisible hands grabbed his legs and pulled him under. The few keys he grabbed tumbled from his trembling hands.

The voices in his head, the invisible hands pulling him deeper, and the incredible cold pushed Billy to limits of his sanity. He grabbed the first glint of color he found and kicked hard to the surface. Leaning against the partially submerged door, he never vacillated before inserting the key.

The mechanism clicked and the door swung open.

Billy stepped through and came face-to-face with his doppelganger. The other Billy's dark and sinister eyes gleamed when he smiled. The original Billy was pushed aside, and his evil twin stepped through the door into his world.

The original Billy waded from the other pond. Pine and birch trees lined the shore. Birdsong filled the air. Behind him, the submerged door faded and disappeared. The dead children had gathered, their blank stares and sinister smiles sending chills throughout his body. Wherever he was, there was no way home. He didn't save his parents, nor did he find his dog, Arlo. The finality was real. Death would be his reward for curiosity and loyalty.

The children closed the circle around Billy. Their chant reverberated painfully inside his skull.

"...and we all fall dead."

He had two choices—make a valiant stand or become one of them.

The children reeked of damp, rotting earth and the sweet cloying scent of death. Billy backpedaled when they rushed forward, swinging at the first one and throwing the second one to the ground. Several grabbed his arms, pinning them to his side. Their fangs bit and their claw-like fingers ripped.

The girl with the green eyes watched as the mass of children wrestled Billy to the ground. Billy tried to resist but fear surged through his veins like an infection.

"Help me. Someone, help me."

A warmth spread throughout his body and he grew weak. His attempts to flee became feeble.

"Into the water, my children," the girl said. "Drag him into the water."

Blood dripped from Billy's numerous puncture wounds. The children released him as they sought a better grip. Momentarily freed, Billy tried to stand but his legs failed to give him support. He flung his arms and kicked his legs as fingers dug into his flesh. He didn't want to go back into the water.

"Can anyone help? Please, someone, anyone help me."

He dug in his heels as the children dragged him in. The water gave him a surge of energy. He stood, tossing children from his back, but was only able to take two steps before his knees buckled.

"Help. Help me."

They pushed his head under water.

Voices filled his head like a loudspeaker. Vivid pictures of the Dark One's past flashed through his mind. The Dark Ones remembered the taste of blood and the flesh of the innocent and licked their lips in anticipation. The last door had been opened. Evil was free to roam unfettered between worlds.

Darkness seeped in around the edges. Billy's lungs would soon burst. He found his legs and pushed up. His head broke the surface and he sucked in a mouthful of air. "Help!" he screamed.

Cold, dank water filled his mouth as the children pulled Billy under again. A dark shadow slithered up his body, wrapped around his neck, and pushed at his mouth. He needed to take another breath. His body urged him to open his mouth. The voices begged him to open up.

His head popped to the surface. "Help…"

The dark shadow slid into his mouth and nose. Evil as old as time filled his being, chewing and consuming his innocence. They dragged him deeper and held him under water until he no longer lived, and the Dark Ones devoured his soul.

They waited.

A single tennis shoe floated to the surface, bounced on the waves, and made its way to shore.

The dead don't stay dead long.

-- At a young age, Chris had success winning young author contests and his love for writing continued throughout high school and into adulthood. He is the founder of a local writer's group that has hosted nationally known authors as guest speakers. His short story "Two Bobbies" was selected for inclusion in the Horror Writers Network Anthology, The Gates of Chaos and was published in March of 2021. "Roadkill Surprise ", a werewolf short story of his was included in the summer print edition of the Horror Zine Magazine published in September 2021.

The Blizzard Dilemma
By Barbara Bustamante

On a cold Wednesday morning at 6:30 a.m. on March 2, 1966, in northwestern Minnesota, everyone in the Paul family struggled to get out of their snug cozy beds in the two-story stucco farmhouse. On her way to the kitchen, Frances, the mother, stopped at the foot of the staircase to holler up at her children to get ready for school. They dressed for the day and thundered down the staircase to devour breakfast.

Coming from the barn with his dog, Walter, the father, entered the house and took off his coat and boots. The children bundled up for the block-long walk to the end of the driveway to catch the bus.

"It's warm out," Walter announced. "Hurry up so the bus driver doesn't have to wait."

The lack of wind felt comforting on the children's faces as they stepped out of the house and walked down the driveway. They boarded the bus and were on their way.

Meanwhile back in the house, Frances watched from the double windows facing the driveway to make sure the children made it to the bus on time. She returned to the kitchen to serve a leisurely breakfast of sunny-side-up eggs, bacon, and toast.

Walter had already poured a cup of coffee when Frances trotted back into the kitchen. He stirred the cream in his coffee. "Do you need to go to town today for anything?"

"No, not today, I have ironing and mending to do," she replied.

"We can go tomorrow when I pick up a part for the grain drill."

He turned on the radio because it was time for the farm report. The announcer focused on the weather, reporting that snow had started falling in Southern North Dakota, moving in a northeasterly direction with winds at 30 MPH. He continued with a long list of school closings which included Fertile/Beltrami, where the children went to school.

The bus turned around at the Beltrami Elementary School to bring the children back home when the driver learned of the storm closing. This day hadn't turned out as everyone had envisioned. Frances and Walter cut their breakfast short with plans to make preparations in the barn and a hefty lunch for a bunch of hungry kids.

Walter headed back to the very large barn whose one side held beef cattle and the other side held the milk cows. Each group of cows separately got water from the stock tank on the south side of the barn while he spread straw bales for bedding and hay for the cows to eat. After the cows returned, he fueled up both the car and the tractor and parked them in the barn. He wanted to be prepared since March could be an unpredictable month when it came to storms. No sooner had Walter parked both vehicles than the school bus stopped at the end of the driveway and dropped the children off. He then returned to the house for a cup of coffee.

Before long the house bustled with the sound of children as they changed out of their school clothes. The younger children raced downstairs to be the first to pick out the best program from three TV channels. The aroma from a huge pot of chili filled the kitchen while Frances and one of the older girls prepared lunch.

By that time the snowfall increased, and the wind picked up speed. Outside, the snow formed thick clouds of white swirling blankets, building flake by flake into massive domes. With winds at 40-50 MPH, it became difficult to see across the yard. By nighttime nothing was visible and all that could be heard was the howl of the wind through the trees and around the buildings.

Inside, the younger children settled down to watch cartoons on TV as Walter and Frances huddled around the radio to learn any news about the storm.

Walter inquired, "Is there any toast and jelly to go with my coffee?"

Frances opened a bag of bread and dropped a slice in the toaster. She opened the refrigerator door and grabbed the jar of jelly.

"Guess what! We ran out of butter." For a moment they just looked at each other, searching for something to say.

Walter broke the silence. "I sure hope this storm is over soon so we can make a quick trip to Beltrami."

"The kids won't like this, especially Janice."

Their pre-teen daughter sauntered into the kitchen. "Did someone say my name?"

"We're out of butter."

"Oh, no, what are we going to do? You know I need butter."

"We'll just have to wait out the storm and get some in town."

After lunch, Frances and Walter noticed the storm was not letting up. Walter anticipated the evening milking.

Frances asked, ""What do you think of the idea of making butter from our cream?"

"Do you know how to make butter?" Walter inquired. "When I was a kid, my older sisters made it, but I never saw them do it. I think they used a churn. We haven't had one of those for years."

"It won't hurt to try. Why don't you take this covered pail and bring back some cream from the milk house tonight?"

"Sure, we'll give it a try." He agreed and headed off to the barn.

Walter returned for supper with the pail of freshly separated cream. Frances put it in the refrigerator. After supper while everyone else watched TV, Frances poured the cream into a bowl. She turned on the mixer and let it run … and run.

Drawn by the noise, the eldest daughter Barbara wandered into the kitchen, "What are you up to, Mom?"

"Dad and I decided to try and make butter since this blizzard is not ending anytime soon," she declared.

"So, how do you do that?"

"I'm trying the mixer, first. Someone told me that when whipping cream do not go beyond stiff peaks or it will turn into butter."

The mixer continued running. The cream turned to stiff peaks, so she let the mixer run longer. And after a while the peaks were gone - still no butter. So, she poured it into a jar and put it in the refrigerator for the night. She vowed to try again the next day.

On day two of the storm, everyone awoke to the blizzard in full force. They were grateful that no heat or power was lost during the night.

The fact that there was no school brought the children one by one to the breakfast table.

The 9-year-old daughter Sandra searched every inch of the table before yelling -" Where's the butter!!!"

"We're out." explained Frances.

"But I have to have butter on my toast."

"You'll just have to do without until the storm is over."

"Can't you drive across the road to Irving's place and borrow some? "

"We can't see across the yard, let alone see the road going to Irving's. I don't even know if they have extra butter and I'm not about to pay long distance phone charges to find out."

Growing up on a farm was a lot of hard work, but it left plenty of time for learning to get along. Barbara and Janice argued over dishwashing techniques. The younger siblings battled on the living room carpet – the boy playing with the dog and the girl dancing the latest rock tune. During the blizzard, no matter what they were doing, all wondered about the butter situation.

Frances took the jar of cream from the refrigerator and glanced at Janice who was rolling her eyes. "I don't know if it will work, but we can give it a try." She dumped the cream into the blender and turned it on – first slow and then a little faster. She stopped and checked to see if it was beginning to turn. No such luck. She turned the blender back on and picked a higher speed and let it run some more. She checked again. Still just cream. She sighed and poured the cream back into the jar for another night.

The next morning was the third day without butter and the storm was not letting up.

Walter said, "I've never seen drifts this high in the 50 years that I've lived here."

"It'll sure take forever to shovel a path to the barn and the poor cows will have a hard time getting to the stock tank," Barbara added.

After doing the baking and cleaning, the girls helped their mother do some spring cleaning. Barbara finished cleaning the bookcase and checked the encyclopedia to see if there was anything about making butter. She sauntered back to the kitchen. "Well, there's nothing in the encyclopedia about making a jar of butter – just how the factories make butter with commercial equipment, "she reported.

Frances decided to make a macaroni hotdish with canned tomatoes and ground beef for lunch.

"I'll start frying the hamburger. You go get the tomatoes and onions in the basement," she instructed Janice.

When Janice returned with the tomatoes, onions, and a can of tomato soup, Frances asked, "Is the soup for yourself again? If you weren't such a good cook, I wouldn't put up with your quirky menu changes."

"You know I don't like tomatoes and onions," Janice answered.

During lunch she commented, "I'll be so glad when we have butter again. I'm tired of putting bacon grease on my toast in the morning."

"Lard tastes yucky on bread," her younger brother added.

"Now! Now! We'll just have to do without butter until we can go to town. I did it as a kid and so can you," Walter interjected.

After the lunch dishes were done, Frances got out the jar of cream once more. While the rest of the children were busy with their afternoon chores, she took her bowl of cream and repeatedly stirred the cream with a large spoon, determined that one way or the other, she was going to make butter. After an hour all she had was a bowl of cream. Running out of ideas, she resorted to pouring the cream back into the jar. But this time she thought that maybe cold cream didn't work. Maybe it needed to be warm. She set the jar on the counter, resigned to attack this problem the next day.

The morning of the fourth day it had stopped snowing and the wind wasn't blowing as hard. No one could see anything outside of the windows except mountains of snow, and the kids wondered how they would make it to the barn. Everyone was also getting tired of being pent up in the house for four days without any butter.

After Barbara finished her barn chores and breakfast, she removed the dishes from the table and filled both sinks with hot water. Frances joined her to gaze out the window.

"Look how beautiful blue the sky is – not a cloud in sight. I just love the shadows as they peek through the trees," Frances said. "The snow is so fresh and white." She picked up the jar of cream and pondered all her efforts. "I just don't know what it will take to turn this cream into butter."

Janice joined them and pointed toward the road. "Look, what's that? Is that the snow plow headed toward our driveway?" She turned and ran to tell her father in the living room. Soon there was a buzz through the house as they all peered out the windows to catch a glimpse of the plow.

In all the excitement Frances flicked her wrist and the cream sloshed from one end of the jar to the other, instantly forming into a solid mass. In response, she grumbled, "Fine time to turn to butter, now that I can go to town."

--Barbara Bustamante holds a BUS Degree in Food and Nutrition from North Dakota State University. She is semi-retired and lives in Moorhead, MN with her cat.

Blizzard in North Dakota March 2-5, 1966

Impacting Humans, Livestock & Economics

By Eileen Tronnes Nelson

Thank You: Christopher Atkinson, Geography Department
University of North Dakota, Grand Forks, ND

PRE-BLIZZARD

January 1966
• Low temperatures all month
• High of 18, low of -33 degrees
February 1966
• Early February: 15 to 25 degrees
• Mid-February: 0 to -25 degrees
• Late February: 20 to 30 degrees
(https://www.ncdc.noaa.gov/cdo-web/)

WEATHER DAYS BEFORE THE BLIZZARD

• Three days before: High temps were 36, 35, and 39 degrees
• Day after first night of snowfall: High of 30 degrees
(https://www.ncdc.noaa.gov/cdo-web/)

LOCALS EXPECT GOING INTO BLIZZARD

• Weather Bureau issued a preliminary warning on February 28, 1966
• March 2, 1966, a severe weather bulletin broadcast on radio and
television
• People canceled long distance travel
• Moved cattle to farmsteads

(Ramsey, Douglas, and Larry Skroch, *One to Remember: The Relentless Blizzard of March 1966*; Grand Forks, ND; Valley Heritage, 2005, Print.)

RESIDENT'S CONTEXT
• Grand Forks played in basketball tournament in Grafton
• Police worked 34-hour shifts
• Almost half of the people in U.S. were under the age of 26
• Vietnam War going on during this time
(Ramsey, Douglas, and Larry Skroch, *One to Remember: The Relentless Blizzard of March 1966*; Grand Forks, ND; Valley Heritage, 2005, Print.)

ELK VALLEY FARMS
• Elk Valley Farms is a bonanza farm owned by the Larimore family.
• During the relentless blizzard of March 2-5, 1966, I lived with my four young children, Douglas (6), Dwight (5), Deborah (3), and Julie (2), and my then-husband, on an Elk Valley farm site, 1-1/2 miles south of Larimore along ND State Highway 18.
Sources: Elk Valley Farm Records, CFL, UND Special Collections & Eileen Tronnes Nelson

FARMSTEAD, ALONG HIGHWAY 18, 1-1/2 MILES SOUTH OF LARIMORE, ND
Source: www.google.com/maps

BLIZZARD BEGAN WEDNESDAY, MARCH 2, 1966

• Snow began in the southern half of North Dakota on Wednesday morning, March 2, 1966, and spread northward by Thursday, March 3, 1966, to all of North Dakota, exceptthe extreme northwestern and north central portions.

• By Friday, March 4, 1966, all parts were in a severe blizzard except the three extreme northwestern counties

Source: U.S Dept. of Commerce, Storm Data, March 1966, Vol. 8. No. 3.

March 2, 1966: Wednesday morning snow beginning in the southern half of ND. Relentless winds.

Source: National Oceanic and Atmospheric Administration (NOAA) Central Library.

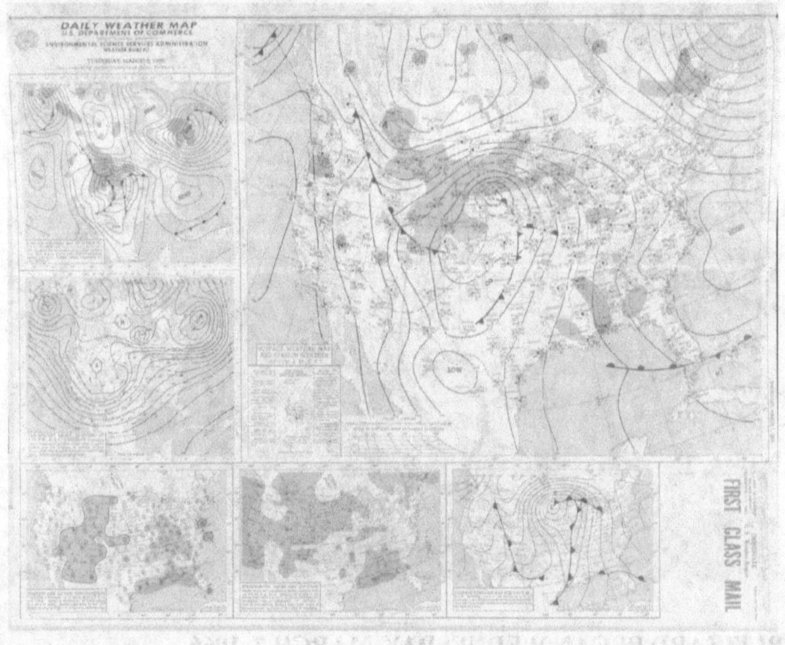

March 2, 1966. Snow spreading to central & northward in ND. Relentless winds.

Source: National Oceanic and Atmospheric Administration (NOAA) Central Library.

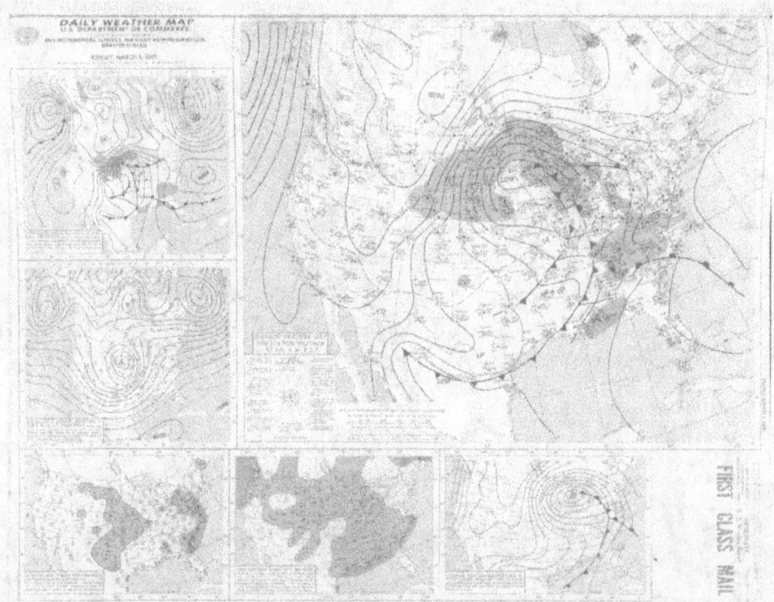

March 3, 1966: Snow covering most of ND. Blizzard. Visibility 1 quarter mile or less for over 30 consecutive hours, up to 100 mph relentless winds during March 3-5, 1966.
Source: National Oceanic and Atmospheric Administration (NOAA) Central Library.

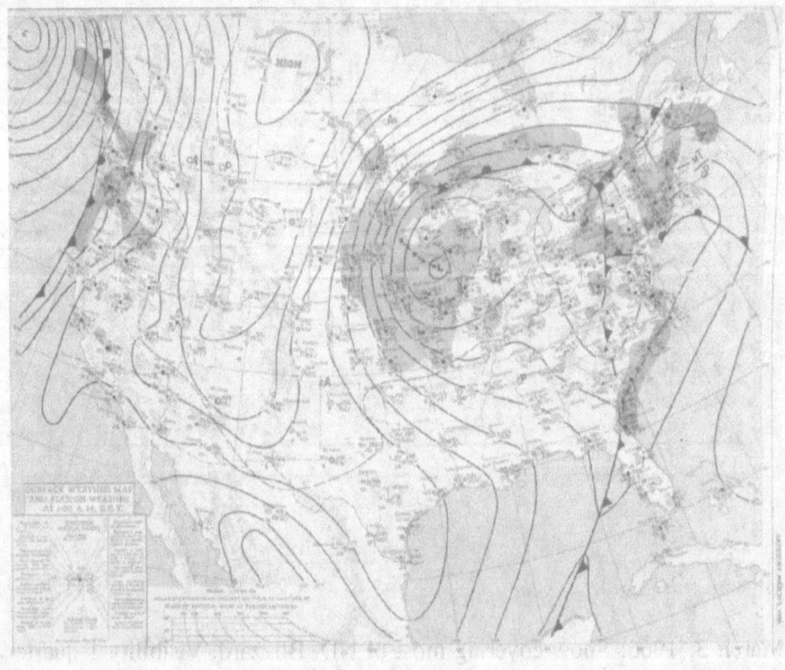

March 4, 1966, Snow covering most of ND. Blizzard.

Visibility 1 quarter mile or less for over 30 consecutive hours, up to 100 mph relentless winds during March 3-5, 1966.

Source: National Oceanic and Atmospheric Administration (NOAA) Central Library.

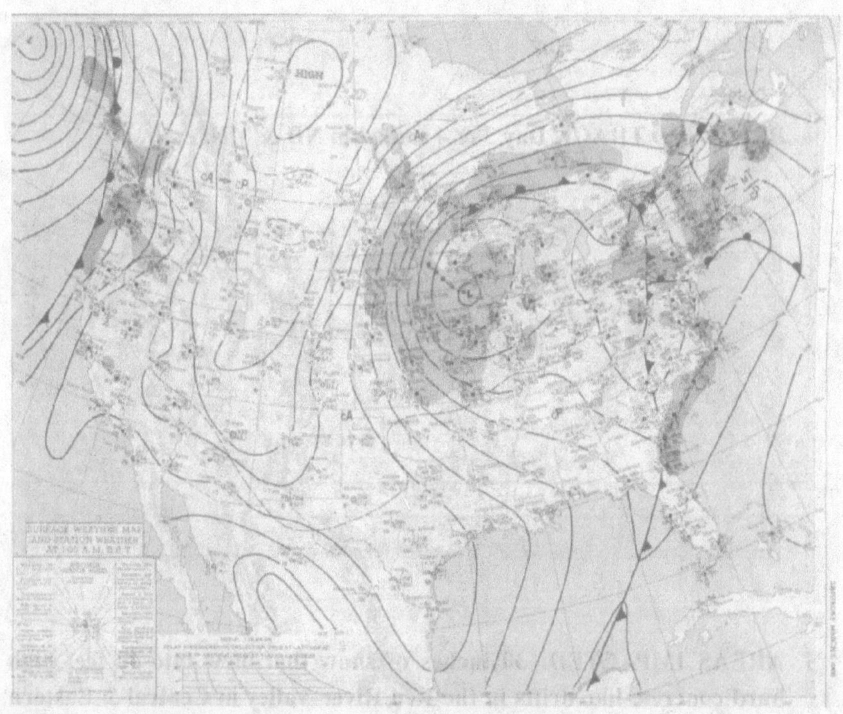

March 5, 1966, the Colorado low-pressure system began to move out of North Dakota.
Source: NOAA Central Library

BLIZZARD TRACK Day 3 & 4 stalled in ND & MN.

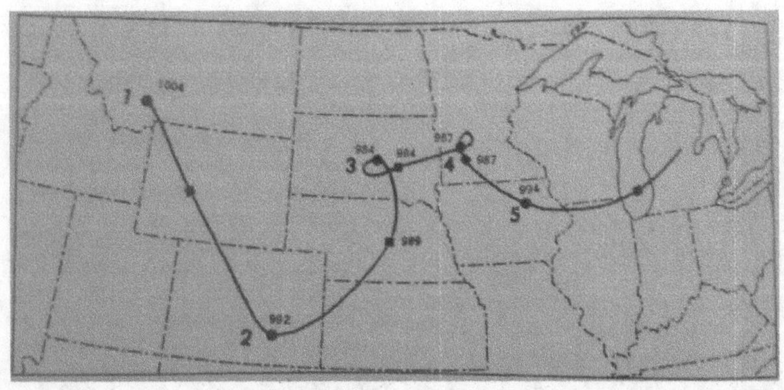

AREAS IMPACTED: 30 inches of snow that blew into 40 feet high hard concrete-like drifts in the Red River Valley in Central & Eastern ND & 30-20 inches in Central MN.

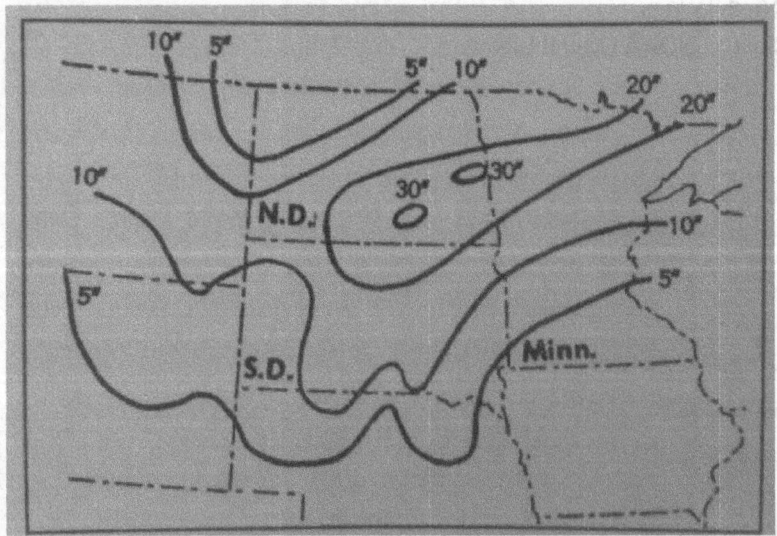

SNOW AND ICE AMOUNTS

Station: BISMARCK MUNICIPAL AIRPORT, ND US GHCND:USW00024011

| Preliminary | Year | Month | Day | Temperature (F) | | at Observation | Precipitation(see **) | | | | At Obs Time |
| | | | | 24 hrs. ending at observation time | | | 24 Hour Amounts ending at observation time | | | | |
				Max.	Min.		Rain, melted snow, etc. (in)	Flag	Snow, ice pellets, hail (in)	Flag	Snow, ice pellets, hail, ice on ground (in)
	1966	3	1	34	5		0.00		0.0		T
	1966	3	2	29	22		0.32		3.4		T
	1966	3	3	22	11		1.24		15.5		8
	1966	3	4	18	8		0.26		3.5		17
	1966	3	5	22	5		0.00		0.0		18
	1966	3	6	18	-11		0.00		0.0		18
	1966	3	7	30	0		T		T		15

WINDS UNABATED FOR FOUR DAYS
• The winds roared furiously for four days and nights.
• Winds were relentless and gusted to 100 mph.
• Visibility remained at zero for 11 hours on March 3, 1966, from 1:00 a.m. until 1:30 p.m.
• Winds caused drifts up to 40 feet.
Source: U.S. Dept. of Commerce, Storm Data, March 1966, Vol. 8, No. 3.

VISIBILITY ZERO FOR 19 HOURS
• Until 7:00 p.m. on Friday, March 4, 1966, the visibility varied from zero to
not more than one-eighth of a mile.

• For a continuous period of as long as 19 hours, visibility was one-eighth of a mile or less and was without known precedent in North Dakota weather history.

Strommel, H. G. 1966. "The Great Blizzard of '66 on the Northern Great Plains." Weatherwise,

19(5): 188-193, 207.

1966 BLIZZARD WORST TO HIT NORTH DAKOTA

• Long stay across the state (3 days)

• Snowfall accumulation (20-40 inches)

• High wind speeds (70 mph with gusts to 100 mph)

Source: State Historical Society of ND, Unit 7: Set 5: 1966 Blizzard

http://history.nd.gov/textbook/unit7_prettygood.until7_5_66 blizzard1.html

HUMAN IMPACT: DEATHS

• 5 North Dakotans died due to some related effect of the blizzard.

• 2 were young girls who died tending to livestock.

• 3 men died of heart attacks while shoveling snow or walking in the blizzard.

• 18 died in three states: ND, SD, and MN.

Source: U.S. Dept. of Commerce, Storm Data, March 1966, Vol. 8, No. 3.

FARM ECONOMIC IMPACT

• 74,500 head of cattle perished.

• Some livestock were in open fields where snow blinded them, causing them to drift into fences where they died.

• The livestock was valued at $12,000,000.

• 2,400 hogs and numerous other animals, such as sheep and turkeys, perished in the storm.

(Ramsey, Douglas, and Larry Skroch, *One to Remember: The Relentless Blizzard of March 1966*; Grand Forks, ND; Valley Heritage, 2005, Print.)

SCHOOLS & BUSINESSES SHUTDOWN

• The shutdown caused a loss to businesses.

• Schools closed to the delight of children.

• Emergency vehicles were unable to respond.

(Ramsey, Douglas, and Larry Skroch, *One to Remember: The Relentless Blizzard of March 1966*; Grand Forks, ND; Valley Heritage, 2005, Print.)

ROADS CLOSED

• Some roads were not cleared for two weeks.

• I could not drive out of the farm site for about two weeks after the blizzard.

• One snow draft blocked a road for half a mile.

Source: Eileen Tronnes Nelson

"WORLD IS COMING TO AN END"

• The blizzard of March 2-5, 1966, on the Northern Great Plains was unbelievable and something I had never experienced before or since that March blizzard.

• I thought the world was coming to an end because of the howling winds that began at noon on Wednesday, March 2, 1966, and ended Saturday, March 6, 1966.

Source: Eileen Tronnes Nelson

RELENTLESS HOWLING WIND

• I would go to bed and the wind was howling. The wind continued to howl during the night. I tried to sleep, and the wind would wake me up. If I did sleep, when I woke in the morning, the wind was still howling. This went on for three nights and four days.

• Additionally, the visibility was zero outside. It was a frightening claustrophobic feeling.

Source: Eileen Tronnes Nelson

ROAD BLOCKED. ELECTRICITY STAYED ON

• North Dakota Highway 18 was blocked for many days, and I do not believe that anyone drove on that highway during the blizzard.

• The electricity stayed on and so did the party-telephone line locally owned by the Elk Valley Farms. The telephone would sometimes not work during high winds, but fortunately stayed on during the blizzard.

Sources: Eileen Tronnes Nelson

"IT LOOKED LIKE THE STORM MISSED US"

• On Wednesday, March 2, 1966, a Larimore woman working downtown, turned on the radio at noon, and heard a storm was sweeping across North Dakota. She looked out the window and commented, "It looks like the storm missed us". She was not seen again until Sunday (four days later). Source: *Larimore Pioneer*, Owners/Operators/Editor/Publishers Bob & Marcie Lind, March 9,1966, BLIZZARD OF '66 EXTRA!, p.1.

From 1961 to 1968, Bob and Marcie Lind owned and operated the Larimore Pioneer in Larimore, ND. On Saturday, March 5, 1966, Bob was out taking photographs after the blizzard. He said he could have used 50 reporters and a hundred photographers to cover this storm. All photography had to be confined to Larimore city because it was impossible to get out of town. Unfortunately, they ran out of regular film; a new supply was somewhere on a snowbound train between his supplier in LaCrosse, WI and Grand Forks, ND. Bob bought some other film downtown and Bob and Murrey Kjorness, the camera operator, fired away, hoping the camera was set properly for that type of film. He wanted to catch the scenes as quickly as possible before the plows got into the act; and besides, they did not have time to process for the special edition after Sunday. Bob Lind produced a special edition, "BLIZZARD OF '66 EXTRA!,'' on March 9, 1966.

Bob Lind joined *The Forum* in 1969 and had been a copy editor, night editor, assistant editor, and features writer. He retired in 1998 but continued to write *The Forum's* popular "Neighbors' feature several times a week. In April 2021, Bob had a stroke resulting in several complications. He passed away in August of 2021.

YOUTUBE VIDEO
• "1966 DEVILS LAKE NORTH DAKOTA"
https://www.youtube.com/watch?v=DGbhZoXWaec

STANDING TALL PICTURE
North Dakota Department of Transportation employee, Bill Koch, taken by ND DOT employee, Ernest Feland on March 9, 1966. Source: https://www.weather.gov/fgf/blizzardof66

-- Eileen Tronnes Nelson, lives in Grand Forks. Graduate of the University of North Dakota and Moorhead State University. Certified Paralegal® National Association of Legal Assistants, retired after serving nearly 40 years at Central Legal Research, School of Law, UND, Grand Forks, ND. I enjoy spending time with my two sons & two daughters, six grandchildren & three bonus grandchildren, three great grandsons, & in-laws: daughter-, son-, three grandsons-, two granddaughters-. I am researching Scandinavian genealogy & writing my historical non-fiction "Settlers in America" series of six books on how I found my Swedish & Norwegian ancestors. Including the brutal murder of Marie Wick; asphyxiation of Eleanor Thompson; documents of Johnson & Tronnes property; and in 2018 travelling in Sweden & Norway with my granddaughter, Jasmine M. Nelson. Additionally, I am writing non-fiction books about the murder of Dianne Bill; Flood of 1997; COVID-19; Domestic Abuse; Genealogy of Living Family; Greed; & UND. AuthorEileenTronnesNelson@gmail.com